Lessons in Demoralization by Nikki R. Leigh

Edited by Jay Alexander.

"That Time I Swallowed a Genie" first published April 2021 as an independent short story by Eerie River Publishing.

"Mr. Giggles" first published November 2022 as an independent short story by Crystal Lake Publishing.

"Win Big or Get Dead" first published October 2021 in Pulp Harvest by Blood Rites Horror.

"On the Same Wavelength" first published October 2021 in Books of Horror Community Anthology Vol. 3, part 2 by RJ Roles.

"The Prop" first published July 2021 in Welcome to the Funhouse by Blood Rites Horror.

"Give to Take" first published May 2021 as an independent short story by Crystal Lake Publishing.

LESSONS IN DEMORALIZATION

Nikki R. Leigh

DARKLIT
PRESS

Content Warning

The stories that follow may contain graphic violence and gore.

Please go to the very back of the book for more detailed content warnings.

Beware of spoilers.

To Mom, my best friend since birth.

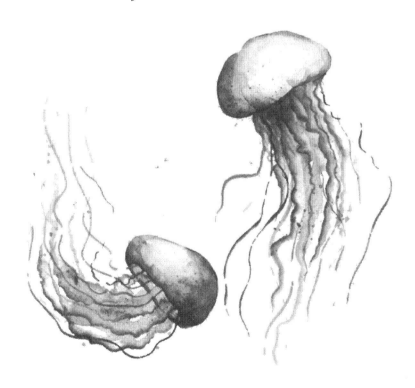

CONTENTS

INTRODUCTION

Making a person is physically simple, once you understand the constructs, physiology, and anatomy of a complex organism. The factory has that down to a science, leaving us with nothing to do but pull levers and move the line along to make anew.

Hands connect to arms, stumps brittle and bloodless. Those arms reach around and find purchase on a torso. The legs are next, small branches of skin and bone and muscle. To top it all, a head, empty for the moment except for the electrical wiring that will help the body move.

The body, the functionality, that's the easy part. But the mind, we've only just begun to figure that out.

What we do know, however, is the power of a story. The morality of it all. The dos and don'ts, the once upon a times, the happily ever afters, and the never ever do what they dids.

Our factory creates, but it also absorbs. Ear horns protruding from the factory roof stretch across the sky, listening, documenting, taking in the stories and journeys and difficulties of the world and out of this world, and placing them into the smallest of worlds to be regurgitated back into society.

Transcriptionists, hands always moving, always writing, saturating pages with ink. The lifeblood of it all. Those pages, those stories, flutter about our factory, siphoning through pipes and into the husks of our children.

The stories we siphon into malleable minds teach us to make, to break, to transform on some fundamental level. Create from anew, desecrate and demolish into minuscule relevance, or some combination of both.

A head fills with a page, and the information is stored. Every head, every story, every cautionary tale. Every lesson in demoralization.

These are those stories. Some process grief through anger, hatred, violence. Others prove whimsical and light in the face of tragedy.

Heed them, forget them, rejoice in them. We help to teach, but not all will listen.

Your choice.

Part One: To Make

RECIPE FOR A DISASTER

1 cup of soil, grave fresh
3 adult teeth (ground)
½ cup of blood

    i.   *Combine blood and soil into mixing bowl. Stir until blood boils. Sprinkle tooth powder. Mix evenly.*
    ii.   *Spread over surface.*
   iii. *Give it a hand.*

The bottom of the well is muddy, only an inch of water beneath her feet. It's barely enough to cover her toes, but God, does it reek. She probably does too, the stench of her actions clouding around her like fog coalescing down a shadowed alley. The darkness of the well comes with a dampness, a humidity that fills her lungs with a rich, soiled smell, a rot of weight in her chest.

How long has it been?

"Well, now, sweet Dez," he had croaked to her. "After you mix and plant the ingredients, you just holler on up, you hear? I'll do my little thing. You hang out down that there little hole, and I promise it'll be your Melinda pulling you back up again in three days."

Three days. That's right.

He had tipped his black top hat at her, winking as he did so. He had told her there were bad things coming—coming quickly—and that she had a choice. Fight her battle on the surface with Melinda ("You'll be sure to perish that way, what with what's coming and all," he'd said) or take her chances in the well and be part of something special ("You might perish down there when all's said and done, but I'll keep Melinda safe," he'd said, shrugging his shoulders at her predicament.)

There wasn't much of a choice, as far as she was concerned, what with the knife held against Melinda's throat. So down she had gone, with her gathered ingredients and his infernal recipe. And down she's stayed. Dez brings a shaking, dirty hand, wet soil stuck under her fingernails, to her forehead, moving her oily hair from her face. She tries to count the suns she's seen rising overhead, a pinprick of light then dark then light again. She's sure there's been two spots of brightness—two days passed. And now, the third is rising. The blood loss has long since deteriorated her ability to think properly, and she stopped examining her fresh stump of a wrist sometime the previous day.

She has ignored the other items at the bottom of the well, taking up residence in the murky wet ground. A mixing bowl, a mortar and pestle, a blowtorch. Some towels. The hellish concoction that has seeped into the ground underneath her feet. Her left hand, detached and laying in the liquid, turning a terrible shade of gray.

He gave her a day to collect the materials. Told her he had a bone to pick with what that recipe would bake. That whatever sprang from the earth below her feet would help him take control of it all.

She remembers, her fatigued mind replaying the scenes of each item's gathering, hoping she's done it correctly. She knows she'll find out soon. She'll find out if something comes forth. She'll find out if she will see her sweet Melinda lowering the rope for her. But knowing she'll find out soon doesn't stop her from churning the memories, picking apart the details like a grain in a film.

1 cup of soil, grave fresh

She'd scoured the local cemetery first. Dez knew this cemetery—it's where her mother was, withering into bones and leathered flesh. She didn't know if the recipe called for the soil of a new grave, or just soil from a grave, dug fresh, so she gathered both in one fell swoop.

She went to her mother. Ran her hand across the cold tombstone and wept. With her other hand, she dug. No shovel, just nails into grass. She dug her hands into the dirt, praying to God her soul wouldn't be cursed by wrongdoing.

The soil clumped at the bottom of a bag. Soil from a fresh grave. She placed a few more scoops of the soil into the bag she'd brought with her, the weight dragging her heart into her legs, slowing her steps. Even in death she couldn't bear to leave the comfort of her mother's presence.

3 adult teeth, ground

When the man came to Dez and Melinda, they were enjoying an evening of beer and reading on their back porch. They'd been laughing at their cat, which was meowing at them from the window though they'd only just escaped to the backyard. The laughter stopped abruptly when he appeared before them, having walked through their side gate.

The women's hands went to the air as he waved his knife about. He apologized for disrupting their evening, told them he'd had them in mind for his task, that he had big goals—

Goals of power. They'd struggled, tousling each other about the backyard when Dez gained a burst of energetic courage, adrenaline coursing through her veins. With the energy of a raging fire she rushed the man in the middle of his tirade. Decked him across the face with the thick book she had in her hand. Loosed a handful of his teeth which he spat from his mouth.

He was angry—that was to be expected when one suddenly has bleeding gaps in their gums. He was angry that she had fought back, despite the threats to her partner.

But his anger vanished quickly, his eye still on the prize.

"Well, that takes care of that," he'd said to her, picking his teeth up from the ground. "I'll hang onto these while you gather the rest. No need to waste fresh ingredients."

And he'd walked away, Melinda in tow by threat of the knife in his hand. He gave her the recipe and directions to the well. Told her she best be back soon, as he wouldn't have his plans derailed by tardiness.

Dez wasted no time.

½ cup of blood

The blood… Dez figured she could collect the blood when it came time to put everything together. She knew her hand would have to go. When the man read the recipe to her, he looked pointedly at her hands, clenched at their sides when he recited the last line: *give it a hand.*

So the blood would come.

And it did.

Dez had lowered herself into the well and spread the materials around her. Baggies of soil, a bowl, a saw. She admired them all, shining back at her. She didn't know what they'd bring, except potentially her freedom. Her mind was frantic at her separation from Melinda. Her own safety be damned—and she suspected it would be—Melinda's life was worth her own.

As she got everything set the way the recipe indicated, a shadow fell over her, blocking what little light was offered by the pinprick circle at the top of the well. The man had returned. An item whistled past her ears, landing with a soft tuft of air at her feet. Dez bent to inspect the bag, identifying the teeth she'd knocked loose what felt like weeks ago.

"No dilly-dallying," the man asserted from above.

Dez complied. She ground the teeth to dust, a process that sapped the energy from her bones, her full weight behind the pestle as it broke the teeth down. Lucky for her, they were rotten teeth from a rotten man. They ground down in due time, leaving her with something resembling a dust, coarse with some bigger pieces mixed in. It'd have to do.

She opened the baggies of soil, took in their damp smell, swearing that she caught a hint of her mother's perfume as she dumped the contents into the bowl.

She looked at the saw. Then at her left hand. Back at the saw.

Feeling her wrist for the space between bones, she scratched a line into her skin where she knew separation would be easiest. She laughed.

Ha, easiest way to remove a hand.

She gripped the saw with her right hand. Adjusted the blade. Wedging. Readjusting. Screaming.

It didn't feel good. But the pain of losing Melinda, of knowing what she had to do and not doing it simply because *it hurt*, motivated her arm to keep sawing back and forth, betraying its twin.

In time—a long, excruciating time—the saw plunked into the ground at the bottom of the well, having completed its course through her skin, her muscles, her tendons, and between bones as much as she could make it.

She held her bleeding stump over the mixing bowl, approximating a half cup of blood through bleary, reddened eyes, blood vessels shot. She dripped over the soil.

"Head's up," he called from above. A blowtorch landed at her knees. "Can't have you bleeding out before you've baked the goods."

She sealed her wound, pain nothing but a numbness against the backdrop of her uncertain future and her desire to see Melinda unharmed. Giving this deranged man what he thought he wanted so she could get out and get safe.

She stirred the blood and soil together, making a thick batter of red-brown mud. She sprinkled the teeth into the mixture, bits of teeth under her nails as she stirred it together, like a recipe for brownies with peppermint crumbles. The mixture soon bubbled under her whisking.

Stir until blood boils.

Her own, within her veins, most certainly was.

She cleared the ground at the bottom of the well. She placed her detached hand into shallow well-water, the murkiness covering the first section of digits. She dumped the mixture on top, spreading it evenly per the instructions.

She groaned something to the man waiting above. He heard her and began his recitation of a spell with words she couldn't make out. The distance too far, the blood loss too much, the pain too great, the separation and despair and contemplation overpowering.

She waited.

It's the third day. Dez is on her back in the well, watching the circle of light get brighter, signaling the rising of the sun. The water, mud, and blood have saturated her back. Her lips are chapped. Her stump throbs angrily. She doesn't know how she's alive. Doesn't know how he expected her to live. He probably didn't. He knew what he wanted, and he forced it upon the world. Her world.

Dez cackles at the sky, delirious with fear. Her mind no longer plays the images of her completing the recipe but instead watches home movies of her and Melinda. Making up scenes of reunion and happy tears.

Like the few times before, the man's shadow casts darkness over the well. The shadow of a man who'd wager his soul for the death of a world.

The ground rumbles beneath her. She scurries to her feet as she hears him clap in delight from above.

"You've served me well, Dez." His voice booms at her, echoing off the walls of the well. It is quickly overcome by the sounds of grating earth below her, the noise bouncing above and below, bouncing around, as the floor of the well erupts.

A hand sprouts from the soil under her feet. She shrieks, a mournful sound that encourages more hands to burst forth until six sets of dirty fingers grasped at the air around her, searching for purchase to push the rest of it (*The baked good*, Dez deliriously thinks to herself) out of the depths of wherever it was born.

Dez backs against the wall of the well, one hand stretched flat against the cold surface, the other a ghost of itself. Her stump thumps against the jagged edges of the stone wall.

A shriek bursts from below.

The six hands belong to one body. One body that slithers from the cracked veneer of the well floor. It has dozens of eyes, a long cylindrical physique. It stares at her.

"Your master! Come meet your master!" the man roars from above.

Dez locks eyes with the thing. *It already has*, she thinks.

It presses itself flush against the walls of the well. She climbs its arms like a ladder. At the top, her eyes blink against the orange sky. She searches the horizon for Melinda.

"Where is she?" she growls at the man.

He grins at her, then taps his head as if trying to remember. "Perhaps I threw her down a well," he sneers.

Dez screams. The creature roars from beside her in the well. Snapping its maw, it rises to its height, twelve feet of writhing flesh.

The man rubs his hands together, excited. "Oh, great creature. You're beautiful. We'll take it all. I called for you, spoke your name into the depths of the well." His mouth curls, pleasure overcoming him. "You're mine."

The creature rears back, its body resembling a cane. It shrieks a high-pitched warning that rumbles into a low bellow, the earth shuddering at its archaic tone.

The giant tubular form jerks forward, like a rubber band pulled to its limit and released.

It eats the man in one bite.

He'd made a fatal error, mistaking his place of power in the invocation. He'd sacrificed nothing save for a few rotten teeth. Dez... Dez had given it all.

The creature had recognized its master. It smelled her sacrifice.

The being gathers Dez in its arms. The two fly through the sky, the orange and red of the horizon surrounding them like fire, enveloping them against the backdrop of impending destruction.

Dez and the creature sniff the air, trying to catch the scent of her lover.

They will find her.

Of that, they know.

THAT TIME I SWALLOWED A GENIE

I thought that passing the tiny urn I'd swallowed a few hours earlier was going to be the worst part of my day. The worst part of my day, to be sure, that would then lead to the best part of my month—selling my stolen goods for that sweet, sweet cash payout. But no, as it turns out, when you swallow something a genie inhabits, that genie still wants out, no matter where his home is located.

I really believed that I was making one of my smarter decisions in life. I was tired of getting caught stealing, but I still really wanted and needed to find some items to boost. Spending a year in prison doesn't make debts go away and I still owed a hefty sum.

Into the pawn shop I went, looking for something accessible, valuable, and worth my time. It was sitting in a jewelry case. The shiny, expensive-looking urn (or was it a jar?) was small enough, about an inch long and a half inch wide, that I thought I could easily get away with it. It had a remarkably small handle on one side—and was that a tiny spout? The hard projections should have been enough to deter my efforts, but I told myself it'd be just like swallowing a chip you hadn't chewed enough.

The pawn shop owner was no doubt trained from years of experience in catching shoplifters to look for the shuffle of a bag, the opening of a coat, the hand too close to the pocket. I was taking a gamble that a subtle well-timed cough wouldn't tip him off. I had the additional advantage of being a petite blonde girl, which certainly seems to strike a little less suspicion around these parts. I had asked to view the urn, along with a couple other items to make it harder for him to remember what I'd asked for. He obliged my request, placing the urn, a few rare coins, and one bracelet onto the countertop. I pretended to hem and haw over the items, and another customer called the shop owner over. *Carrie*, I thought, *it's now or never. Down the hatch!*

Once he was out of sight, I took the urn, got my water bottle ready, coughed loudly—bringing my hand to my mouth—and stuffed the trinket inside. Unlike the rest of my plan so far, the urn did not go down smoothly, and I fought tears as I swallowed, swallowed, and gulped again, trying to get my throat muscles to move it downwards. The air became less and less available to my lungs, and my neck strained with effort, all while I tried to appear inconspicuous as I continued looking at the items, my back turned to the rest of the store so they couldn't see my bulging eyes.

At long last, the urn reached the point of no return and decided it would go down, and relief flooded my mind as I was able to take a breath again. I drank some water to help the tiny metal piece on its journey, and when all was clear, I let out a few bursting coughs, squeezing out an "excuse me" when I could.

The shop owner returned, and I told him I'd pass on the items, but thank you for his time. I walked towards the door, in the clear, and as he walked away I swear I heard a muttered "dirty thief" from his lips. *Ha*, I thought. I'd like to see him prove it.

I made it home, to my trailer in a dark corner of the woods, which I'd inherited from dear old Dad along with his drinking habits and troubles with the law. I opened the door and flopped onto my couch, stained from Dad's previous binging activities, and contemplated the day's work. I was excited to see how much I could get from the urn—once it made itself present *outside* my body, that was. It seemed like a unique piece and I was hoping for a couple hundred dollars. Not bad for a day's work, considering it was just the cherry on top of all the other stuff I'd stolen from cars on the way home.

As I was congratulating myself on my victory, my stomach rumbled loudly, and the urge to relieve myself hit strong. I didn't know if I wanted to throw up or take the biggest dump I could muster. Not wanting to give in just yet, in hopes that it would pass, I rubbed my stomach to try and dull the cramping.

I should have just puked.

Without warning, something burst out of me. Not the something I was expecting from the somewhere I was expecting, but rather a bright flash of light that shot itself straight out of the center of my stomach, through the skin, only to coalesce in front of my face, floating above my living room floor. My skin burned and tingled after the form osmosed its way through my body; never had I felt a fire in the pit of my stomach spread to my throat and through my eyes and down to my toes.

"How can I be of service?" a booming voice asked from the space the bright light inhabited. The light slowly began to focus itself, and standing in front of me was a man, or something like a man, at least. His body had a stout trunk, his legs stiff beneath him. What looked like claws emerged from the tips of his fingers, protruding from his skin, in and out, like those of a cat. And his face, or what might pass for a face, came together in a sharp point: a beak of sorts, with holes on either side of his nose. His eyes, though, were jovial and welcoming.

I tried to ask him who he was but all that came out of me was a strangled mewling noise I had never heard made before.

The man… person… entity smiled at me—however it is you smile with a beak-face—and took my shaking hand between his paws.

"I am Adeel. You seem to have summoned me from my vessel, and I am now in service to you to grant you three things that you desire. And you are?"

A genie. I'd summoned a genie. I shifted, confused and still pained from the urn—oh the urn!

"Uh… I'm Carrie. Did you…did you come from a tiny little jar, about yay high, silver, very little spout and handle?" I asked, my voice conveying the disbelief I felt. At this point, he could either be a genie from the urn-lamp or that small trinket had contained a large amount of lead and I was slowly suffering from poisoning.

"That's the one!" he excitedly responded.

"Why is your lamp so… small?" I asked hesitantly. It's never easy asking a man about the size of his lamp.

Adeel rolled his eyes and took an exasperated breath. "It's like a snail. You know how you don't often see snails when they're itty bitty and have those super tiny, fragile shells? But then all of a sudden BAM, you've got this colony of bigger snails with those crunchy thick homes on their backs? Genies are like that too."

"Oh…" I scratched my head, causing dandruff to fall to my shoulders. Bad habit.

"Snails get older, more experienced at doing snail things, and their shells grow around them. Genies have to start somewhere, so we're usually given a tiny trial lamp, and the more wishes we grant and lives we change, the bigger our lamp gets."

"So you're like, a newbie, then?"

"Fresh outta the energy vortex I was born from. The more I'm able to change the lives of those who summon me, the faster I can move up the ranks. Only granted a few wishes so far, including the owner of that shop you got me from."

"What were his wishes?" I asked.

"A genie doesn't usually like to give those away—makes the wishes impure—but if you must know… he wished for a new car, for his wife to come back to him, and… well, the last wish I just can't quite remember," the genie replied, tapping the side of his strange pin-sized head.

"Okay then," I thought out loud. "Do I, like, get some wishes?"

"You bet! Whenever you're ready, just rub your tummy and I'll be there for you, ready to take your wish order."

I should really have taken the time to contemplate my wishes, to make sure there was no monkey paw business going on with them, but my mind was racing with ideas.

"Well, I have a wish now, if I could ask it, Adeel."

"Sure thing!"

This one was a no-brainer. "I wish that my debts would be erased."

"You got it!" God, this was such a perky genie. Adeel swayed back and forth, his eyes rolling back into his head. I heard a faint *pop* and then he was staring at me again with that smile on his face.

"How do I know that worked?" I asked, unsure of how to proceed.

"Call one of your associates. I'm sure they won't say a word about any debt."

I picked up my cell phone from the sofa seat next to me. I called Cal, the guy I'd been planning to sell my items to.

Three rings, no answer.

"He didn't pick up," I said to Adeel.

"That's because he's dead! HA!" Adeel shriek-laughed.

"Dead? I asked for my debts to be erased, not my creditors to be killed!" I shouted at him.

"A deal's a deal. Debts are gone. I promise it was quick."

I was skeptical. "What's your idea of quick?" I asked.

The genie's eyes lit up with what I suspected to be malice. "A flash fire, burning through a warehouse for Cal. Jen drowned in a bowl of soup. And Malcolm, well... I sent an errant bus his direction."

I wasn't sure how I felt about this. I should be even more careful with my second wish. Even when trying to be clear and straight-forward, that paw had still gotten monkeyed. I didn't like the idea that I was responsible for three deaths, but it was kind of nice to have those debts erased. Maybe this wouldn't be so bad after all.

As soon as I had that thought, it felt as if the universe laughed at me and yelled "Psych!" as my stomach started to rumble yet again. This time, the fire burned intensely, even worse than before. It felt like my insides were beginning to liquify. My fingertips were vibrating, and it felt like the nails were beginning to separate from the rest of each finger. Actually, scratch that, it didn't just feel like it—they were. Bloody rivulets began to run down my arm from my fingers and my stomach screamed in agony. I fell to my knees and groaned.

"So, Adeel," I asked through gritted teeth. "This lamp that I swallowed... is it, like, made of lead?"

Adeel shook his head. "No, no. We're just as sensitive to lead as you are. And iron. Our lamps are made of special material. Come to think of it..." he trailed off, scratching his head. I looked up at him, trying to urge him on. "Come to think of it, the materials we use in our lamp are likely very toxic to you humans. You say it's in your stomach?"

I shook my head as vigorously as I could, though at this point I wasn't sure if it was because of the shaking of my body or voluntary.

"Hmm," Adeel thought out loud. "You should probably complete your wishes soon. I don't think it's a good idea to keep that thing in there."

He was right. Every passing moment was agony. My nailbeds continued to bleed, and it felt like my eyes were bulging out of my face. I didn't want to check to see if they actually were. I guess cosmic genie energy lamps really don't do a body good. I needed to come up with my next wishes quickly, but I could barely think straight through the pain and disorientation. Maybe I could just try and upgrade my life a little. I'd always hated this trailer.

"Uh, I dunno," I stammered. "I wish for a new house."

"Done!" Adeel chirped. His eyes rolled, his body shook, and that *pop* sounded a lot louder this time—closer to my ears, almost inside my head. As soon as the pop resounded, a roar began. I managed to look upward through the skylight in my trailer and saw a huge shadow plummeting towards me. If I didn't know better, I'd say—

CRASH.

A new house literally fell from the sky. The wind howled as the house made contact with the ground, absorbing my trailer into its body. Most everything in the trailer was flattened, and splinters of wood made their way towards my face. I covered up and huddled as debris flew all around me.

"Christ, Adeel! Was there no way to do that, I dunno, more smoothly?"

"Sorry, I'm still pretty new at this. Baby snail, remember?" Adeel looked genuinely sheepish. "Alright, two wishes down. Debts paid, new house. What else can I do for you?"

I didn't know how to respond. The pain continued to mount and I had no clue how to make a wish without disastrous results. That new house had almost killed me, and I was pretty sure that if I didn't make my third wish soon, I'd die of toxic lamp syndrome. I remembered then that the shop owner had somehow survived his three wishes; he was there, after all, for me to steal this lamp in front of. He'd even expressed joy in calling me a dirty thief. Which I was, but that was beside the point. *Wait, he knew I stole that lamp, and he let me walk away. Almost as if he...*

"So Adeel," I started, trying to sound confident through the radiating flames in my gut. "About the wishes the shopkeeper made. Did you screw those up just as good as these?"

"I didn't think so, but I suppose I did."

I pressed on. "He wished for a car?"

"He got a fancy red sports car. Just like his brother's. Actually, it was his brother's and he had left it in his will for the guy. I just sped up the process."

I could see where this next one was going. "And his wife coming back to him? What'd you do, kill the guy she ran away with?"

"Well, actually, she was dead already. I guess you humans aren't as thrilled by people coming out of their graves as I might have thought."

Okay, I guess I didn't see that one coming.

"And his last wish?"

"His last wish was… to get rid of me. As it turns out, I'm very bad at this job."

"And that's when I came in?"

"Yep, and swallowed me down."

So that's how he'd survived this. Got out before things got worse. Smart man. All right, I can do that too. I'll just figure out how to get rid of this lamp inside of me. As I went through various scenarios and wording in my head, a new wave of nausea and torment ripped through my body. At this point, I was pretty sure my eyes were bleeding and, for the second time today, bulging from my head. Except this time, the bulging had turned to full on expulsion. My nose dripped, my mouth filled with the taste of iron and bile. The room rushed around me, turning and turning as the pain reached new heights.

"I wish…" I stumbled to my elbows.

"Speak up!" Adeel shouted, trying to reach me through the thunderous flashes of white searing in my head.

Was I even alive anymore? I could barely utter a wish, let alone think of how to word it just right. Delirium kicked into overdrive, and it felt like my brain was hemorrhaging, along with every other cell in my body.

One shot. One shot left.

"I wish this lamp was out of my body!" I yelled with as much force as I could muster.

I'm sure the genie did his eye and shaking thing, but I couldn't see clearly anymore so I wouldn't know. My ears worked just well enough to hear the loud *pop* indicating the wish being granted, but this pop was accompanied by a rip—and that rip came from my stomach.

The lamp shot out of my midsection, leaving a bloody hole in its wake. It clamored to the floor, and I tipped over onto my side. My vision fluttered in and out.

"Done," Adeel said, kneeling next to me. "Thank you for allowing me to serve you. I feel as though I have changed your life very much and appreciate your sacrifice in allowing me to grow." He gave me one last look before a bright light appeared, flashing as he sank back into his lamp.

I was surrounded by a growing pool of blood and I knew that I had royally screwed that wish up. If I could move, I'd kick myself. It may not have been the best life I could be living, but damn it if I didn't want to keep living it. As things began to fade, and the pain finally dulled as my breathing slowed, I opened my eyes, fixed on the lamp. Maybe if I could reach it again, rub it one more time, I'd get more wishes and I could fix this. I reached out, my bleeding fingers almost brushing its surface.

The lamp vibrated. I wasn't sure if I was hallucinating or not, but in my last moments I swear I could see the lamp inch away, like a snail, leaving a trail of my blood behind it.

GIVE TO TAKE

It's just hair. It'll grow back.

It always does.

When you learn the craft, they don't tell you enough about how important that attachment is—that sacrifice to take something that's a part of you and make it apart from you, tied to a totem or placed in a jar. *You have to take*, they always whisper. *Take from the one that took from you and you give it right back to them.*

What I know is that taking is only half the power; it's the giving that does them in. When I'm doing my magic, I give them everything.

It's a sticky Saturday night, and I've given just about all I have, to make them suffer.

I look in the mirror. My hair is shorn down to the scalp. I snip again and again, taking pieces into my hands and placing them into jars, handkerchiefs, until I'm down to my last lock. *It's just hair*, I repeat, looking at what's left of my long waves, nothing but stumps clipped to erratic heights, leaving me looking like the doll of a possessed child who got ahold of the scissors.

I'm no priestess, but my time in the swamp has had me crafting my magic with one goal in mind: revenge. Those boys came into my home, caused a disastrous mess, leaving my tin trailer in disarray, juvenile epithets scrawled on my walls.

Swamp witch! the walls screamed. *Backwoods monster.*

So that's what I'll give them. I don't need to take from them first. They can keep their hair, their nails, their juices. I've perfected the magic of giving and that's what I'll keep on doing until they've suffered enough. Until they've suffered *all the way.*

With my final locks of hair in their various containers, my magic trapped until I'm ready for it to leech their happiness away, I leave my home.

By the end of the night, I've got my gifts planted in the soil surrounding the homes of those that dared cross the threshold of my house with ill intent. I wait, knowing full well that I'll feel it when it's time.

On Monday, I feel the first time my offerings take. The one who broke my windows and every belonging in my house has an unlucky accident involving a skylight and a tree limb. No one could understand the angle at which that branch fell to cause the damage that it did, but he swallowed that limb all the same, pinned to the floor beneath him like a speared fish.

On Wednesday, my hair sings in satisfaction. It calls to me across the distance, showing me how the boy who scrawled the visceral words on my trailer walls had a nasty encounter with a wasp nest while mowing the lawn. I know he felt every one of those stings, those bites, bringing him the pain that each of his ugly words has brought on me and countless others with every jab.

Thursday brought the disfigurement of the boy that lit the burning cross in my yard in a misguided attempt to impose his God on me. The flames had spread across my lawn, over the vines and moss and bushes that provide shelter to those around me. This boy would burn in return, scarring just enough of his face that he would always be reminded how fire, like magic, gives as much as it takes.

One week from the endowment of my gifts, the last boy who dared raise his ire at me was felled by my intent. This one had seized from me my safety, my pride. His urine in the corner of my room, spread across my bed, onto the pictures of my family—gone from this world now—took my sanity.

So I took his in return: a favor to quell my anger. With his mind gone, lost to the murky landscape of my home, I called back to him. He walked, mind empty, back to my trailer. Walked, walked back to my swamp. Walked off the invisible plank and into the thick, brown waters below, feeding the gators, giving back. I got to see this time, to watch as the gators tore him limb from limb before completely erasing him from existence.

A smile on my face, I strolled back into my trailer and to my mirror, cracked from the boys' brief encounter inside my home. I caught sight of my almost-bald head, smiling at the uneven haircut, wearing my justice proud. Unlike the shearing of my hair, their actions had consequences that would ripple like rain-disturbed water far beyond their time. My reflection grinned back at me as I thought about the power they tried to take from me. But my power was just like my hair.

It always grows back.

TO PLUCK A SEED OF SORROW

I visit the Crying Fields once a week. Tears, absent a body, sprout from the ground as stalks of wheat, and when the breeze shakes the flaccid limbs the sobbing hits its peak. It's a place that's beautiful despite its despair. The wind carries intertwined pain across the landscape like a symphony.

When I first took my clients to the Crying Fields, I attempted to keep it professional; I had no business wallowing in their desperation. But after a year harvesting the wheat, I'd learned the best way to provide true peace was to listen to their stories and plant them accordingly.

It's Sunday, and I'm back. Cresting the hill, I'm pulled closer by the sounds of mourning with my jar in my hand. I stare across the golden field, the wind beating the stalks of wheat into a sharp angle so they're almost laying flat.

I feel the gentle hum of the seed in the jar, ready to speak, waiting for its turn to be planted in the ground.

I twist the lid open and listen to its story.

Sadie Sharpe, Mortician for the Soul. I flipped my business card back and forth in my hands, contemplating if this was the next place I should render my services. The open wake was filled with sad eyes, hunched figures dressed in black, with the occasional flower accent pinned to chests.

I attend as many of these as I can, despite not knowing the characters. I do, however, know the plot. When someone dies violently, much like the death by skydiving accident suffered by Rachel's late husband, Beau, it's only a matter of time before their displaced spirits find their way home, even when their bodies are elsewhere. Rachel will soon hear bumps in the night, the whooshing of curtains from windows unable to remain fully closed. Manifestations. Moaning.

I'm here to try to save her that grief. She has enough of her own to absorb.

I hover by the food, curving and popping my card in my hand. I wait for my opening. Rachel, having sat in the corner for most of the time here, surrounded by friends, expresses her need for a cigarette.

I briskly make my way to the back door, tracing her path and attempting to get there before she does. I've never learned a way to make this greeting more palatable, like I'm not some predator trying to levy my services on those lost in their mourning.

I don't try to explain, knowing that the seeds and the Crying Fields aren't public knowledge, but rather a best-kept family secret. I do, however, hope that when the time comes, the grieving will realize what I can offer them, how I can keep their stories from becoming another long-term American haunting.

Rachel appears through the glass of the back door. I prepare, take a breath, wish myself luck and to not make things more awkward than they are most certainly going to be.

"Oh," she says from the doorway, stepping onto the patio from her sliding glass door. "Do I know you? Or did you know Beau?"

"Neither," I say. "But I'm very sorry for your loss."

Rachel looks to the sky, her eyes vacant, heavy with the exhaustion of bereavement. She doesn't question why I'm here. Perhaps she's thankful for a chance to just exist in a moment, without having to perform her grief in the presence of someone she knows, in the way she expects. The silence, lost in thoughts, faraway stare... a recognizable pattern.

I hand her my card. "Just in case," I say.

"Mortician for the soul?" she asks. They almost always have to see to believe.

"I don't want to overstay my welcome today, but if you think he's here, sometime down the line, call."

Rachel, in her haze, just nods. It's hard to be phased when the unimaginable has already happened.

I take that as my chance to slip away.

Ten days later, my phone rings. I'd be lying if I said I hadn't shot the phone a thousand glances, daring the screen to light up and for a client to call. The need to help aches deep in my heart, to pluck their seed of sorrow from them and grow it into something else that sprouts, with strength and beauty, from the earth.

"Sadie Sharpe," I answer.

"I don't know if you remember me, but my husband died a couple of weeks ago. Beau. This is Rachel." She pauses. "I think he's still here."

"Do you mind if I come over?"

"Whenever you can."

"I'll be there in an hour."

She hangs up, and I grab my keys.

My head rests against the steering wheel as I steel my nerves to enter her home. I've done this a hundred times before, but lately, my soul is worn down. It's hard to carry the burden of the dead, to plant them in the Crying Fields.

My mother and I live next to the Fields. We have for a dozen years. She's the only one who knows of my work, the seeds I've sown. She doesn't visit the Fields, herself. They're mine to tend, my crop of spirits given the freedom to express themselves without harming others.

She may not plant the wheat, but she helps me tend the harvest. Gives me comfort. Bakes bread from the grains that turns the sadness into something warm. I sigh, craving her presence.

Lifting my head from its place on the steering wheel, I turn my car off, walk to the front door of Rachel's house, and knock lightly.

Within seconds, Rachel answers, her eyes rimmed red. She ushers me inside.

"How'd you know?" she asks, breaking the silence.

"Unexpected death always leaves a displacement. Where did he spend the most time?"

"In our son's room." *Jesus… a son. I must have missed that detail.* As if on cue, a sharp *thunk* fills my ears, followed by a howling that seems to come from deepest bowels of the earth. He's angry. They usually are at first. The sadness, where they remain, comes later.

"May I?" I ask. And she nods, lingering at the bottom of the stairs.

"First door on the left. My son is at my dad's for the night. He couldn't… we can't take what we saw."

I understand. "Should just be a few minutes."

I head up the stairs, feel the chill in the air. Taking a breath, I place my palm on the doorhandle, wrap my fingers around it, and push open the door.

I scan the floor first, looking for his seed. I look under his son's bed, waiting for the tiny golden pinprick to stand out against the horizon. Nothing under the bed. I crawl back out, stand up. I feel the static in the air and know that he's arrived.

I turn to check the shelves and am greeted by Beau.

People expect ghosts to look just like the dead they represent. A clean, foggy outline of our loved ones. White or translucent, wisping through the air, hiding in shadows.

Ghosts—spirits—they're emotion. They're raw. They manifest as such. Dripping outlines of a humanoid body, black like the voids of space, churning, crawling with skittering specks. They're wet, making the air abysmally dry around them. They're in focus, then out of focus. They're loud.

My heart jumps, taking in the shape that is Beau. No matter how many times I've seen this before, have come face to face with what's left of a spirit broken by death, it makes me feel my life and my vulnerability in bright surges of terrifying electricity. He lurches towards me. His arm, a crackling stump, slices through my chest. When they touch you, it screams and hurts and burns and leaves a mark on your mind. Yells violently about the hell the other side can be, disrupted from your place on earth and forced to live in a darkness that does nothing but consume.

I push through the disorientation, continuing my search for the seed. I head to his son's desk, where I see a set of cars and trains on the surface. I pick up a train, shaking the small toy, hearing a sound like a pebble in a tin can. From behind me, Beau's ghost screams, a hellish sound that makes your brain tremble behind your eyes.

Like a tiny lump of coal from the hearth of the train, the seed tumbles out into my open palm. The howling continues, and I catch the shape buzzing like a cloud of flies in my periphery. From my bag I grab a small mason jar.

Twisting the jar open, my hand blurring in my manic vision, I drop the seed inside and promptly turn the lid of the jar shut.

The howling stops. Beau is gone.

But from behind his disappearing form, the black spots dancing in the air like gnats over a small pond of still water, something stays. Something translucent, but suggestive in its outline, a wriggling form like the jagged line of an ocular migraine beginning, clouding your vision. Something that swallowed the room with its dread, its simultaneous presence and absence. Something that points. At me. It's almost soundless; only the white noise static of broken air-waves buzzes.

Before I can truly take in its form, it vanishes with a sharp noise like an old TV set shutting off, leaving no trace of its presence except the swell of dread beneath my breast. In all the souls I've taken to the farm, I've never crossed paths with *that*.

I shake the feeling, knowing there's nothing I can do except place the memory in my head should I see it again.

I exit the room and walk back down the stairs. I place a hand on Rachel's shoulder, whose eyes bore into mine, pleading, hopeful.

"It's done."

She nods. Thanks me. Asks not for answers, has no expressible questions.

I head home. When I get there, I go straight to the small farmland and plant Beau's seed in the Crying Fields. His mournful wailing begins when I sink the seed into the earth, and I hope he's able to expend his grief between the comfort of others. He died from a height, so I give him a spot on a hill where he'll never have to hit the valleys below.

Before I leave for a jaunt in the a nearby park, I stop at the house and see my mother bustling about in the kitchen. With her head still in the cabinet next to the oven, I hear her call out.

"Sadie? That you?"

"Who else would it be, Mom?"

"Death, finally come to get an old lady maybe."

I walk behind her as she emerges from the cupboard, loaf pan in hand. "Don't say that," I scold her. "We both know he wouldn't let you go quietly."

She smiles at me, readying her tin with some butter, spreading it over the sides and in the bottom. "Don't be such a jerk," she says playfully.

"I wouldn't know at all where I got that from."

She huffs at me, still smiling. My mom has a playful soul for her sixty years of life. I give her a hug, finding comfort in her hold, her slender shoulders under my hands. For as much as she bakes, she's maintained a slim figure over the years.

"What're you making?"

"Lemon bread. The recent harvest was perfect for the recipe."

"The wheat will always provide," I say somberly.

My mom grasps my shoulder and squeezes. "You know how I feel about what you do, kiddo. Helping the lost find their ground is never something to be glum about."

I purse my lips, unsure of how to reply, remembering the strange figure I saw, willing away the shuddersome image and feeling of foreboding.

"I'm going to the park," I finally respond.

"Looking for seeds?"

"I heard there was a heat stroke death there a few days ago. Figured I'd give it a go. At the very least, I can feed the geese."

My mom smiles gently at me. "They're lucky to have you. Be safe. I love you."

Knowing the fleeting nature of life, we never miss an opportunity to remind each other our love and trust in one another.

"I love you too, Mom. See you later tonight."

I walk the park along its rim, craning my head around beaten paths and spots not immediately noticeable to the untrained eye. The police scanner I'd jotted notes from mentioned an individual deceased from the inclement weather at the park, in an encampment with the location withheld. Individuals experiencing homelessness often camp in the park, seeking shelter in the shade from the woods.

These kinds of death don't always produce a seed, the logic of the death cycle seemingly unable to parse out what truly counts as a sudden death. Constant exposure to the elements like this… a lifetime of bad luck and a system that doesn't have your best interests in mind. Hardly sudden. I'll always argue against whatever is out there determining who gets plucked with no trace and who leaves a seed behind to be harvested, that few people wake up and decide today's the day to die. But alas…

The park isn't large, so I figure it should be easy to spot the encampment. The sun is still high in the sky, but the park is empty, much too hot to enjoy a run or a game of touch football.

After a half hour of walking, almost completely circling the park, I see the vague outline of a tent and a tarp deeper in the woods. I creep about, hoping I'm not about to intrude upon a living person's personal space. As I near, the ragged yellow police tape tells me otherwise.

Emergency response teams have left the encampment behind, likely enlisting the help of community services too backed up to respond promptly. I approach the tent, waiting for signs of the dead to appear.

I hear nothing—no howling. I see no dark form. I rifle through what's left of the site. A few cans, some tattered clothes, an abandoned shopping cart. I don't see a seed anywhere, and there is no spectral form that seems to be roaming either.

Perhaps this one passed on without leaving a displacement behind after all. I sigh, hoping that's the case. The peaceful aftermath of a passing, even one at the end of suffering, is always welcomed in this line of work.

I turn to head back to the park, but freeze as I hear the static, the electricity buzzing in the air. My hair stands up on the back of my neck, the feeling of being watched nagging my skin, calling forth bumps.

I look around. Nothing, just as before. No dead or living.

I turn my attention back to the site one last time, then pivot and walk away.

The electric whine and hum continues, distorting the space around me, but I cannot locate its source. I walk briskly, hurriedly, to my car. Climbing in, I place the keys in the ignition. I turn in my seat, pull out of the space, and my breath hitches.

The translucent *thing* is back, occupying a space that has no location. The void of its form points. It points not with a finger, but with something sickle-shaped, curved and pointed. The outline marks me.

I keep driving, the figure shrinking in my mirror before blinking out of existence.

The dread is back in full force.

I know not what it portends, but I know that I don't want it, whatever it is.

I drive home, my heart and mind heavy. The things I see in the wake of a death certainly weigh on me. I feel their grief, the sadness of those left behind, and I don't take for granted that I haven't yet had to search for the seed of a loved one of my own. I don't know that I'd be able to plant it.

But this form that's appeared twice now to me, recently, *suddenly*, I fear what it means. It doesn't seem to take me, doesn't seem to reach out and grab me in its blurry hands. I've never seen the reaper itself, just what it leaves behind. My chest hammers as I tremble, wondering who it plans to take. I selfishly wish upon the fields of wheat I pass that it isn't me or mine.

"Mom?" I shout, entering our shared home. I smell fresh bread, the lemon scent wafting from the kitchen.

But above that, another scent reaches my nose. Sulfur, rot. The scent of death.

I charge upstairs, hearing the shower running, soon feeling the dampness beneath my feet. I feel as though someone is demolishing the bones in my chest, breaking them down with hammer strikes one after another. Please, not her. Please don't take her yet.

"Mom?!" I yell out, rounding the corner of the bathroom, and nearly slip as my knees lock up in shock.

She's hanging over the tub, blood on the floor underneath her head. A stroke? A heart attack? What happened?

She isn't breathing.

The water is hot, but her skin is cold. I feel for a pulse.

A howl from the kitchen confirms her death.

My own howl replies.

I race back downstairs, frantic to find her seed. Stop her haunt before it truly begins.

The black, hazy form, dripping tar at the kitchen entry, tells me I'm too late. She reaches, I cry; I duck under her outstretched, rubbery, dry form, elongated like the arm of a squid, fried by the sun.

I know where her seed is. I've thought about it, always prepared for the worst.

I open the oven, still warm from the freshly baked bread. It's there, shining, the golden lump inside, and I grip it in my hand. I don't bother putting it in a jar.

I push through my mother's dark, static, wet form, gasping at the shock of derangement that penetrates my body, turning my vision murky.

I don't turn as I leave our home. I don't see the translucent construction that's appeared twice already today standing in the doorway, pointing. I know it's there, as the electricity whines in my head. It came for her, and now it comes for me.

Just a few more minutes until I reach the Crying Fields.

This time, I know the story. I know the characters. I'm familiar with the shocking plot device. I hold her seed in my hand, and still, I listen. The story is expected, just not so soon. Her sadness drips over me, lashing my shoulders and my heart. It spins my mind, a cyclone of anguish, textured by whips of melancholy leaves chipping away my stoic veneer.

With the seed, I cry.

I walk down the side of the hill, tears zigzagging across my face by the force of the wind. The wheat around me bows in reverence. I find her place, at the center of the field. She'll provide warmth to the rest. Always a hearth, that woman.

Dirt fills my hands as I cup the soil into my palm, gently, digging only the requisite depth to plant the seed. The deep golden seed tumbles in the palm of my hand.

My mind is shaking, fabricating her howls of death, mingled with her sobbing made in the departure of her afterlife. As if I can see the sadness, my vision is blue, streaked with deeper cerulean slashes, blinding me.

I place the seed at the bottom of the small hole I created. I bury the seed. My tears, dripping, water it. I'll wait for the seed to grow.

The wind kicks up, rains grain around me, on my knees. Curling up on the ground, cradling my mother's resting place, the wheat falls around me. The wind pushes it flat, over my body, filling the air with wails and sobs. The noise envelops my mind and pushes the very essence of my being to the brink before spilling over.

In my hut of wheat, my enclosure of grief, I wither.

The fields will need harvesting in a couple of days. The wheat will always grow, as bereavement is never complete. They'll never find the space amongst the wheat where my body once lay. I'll never hear them wonder aloud, looking for remains.

There will be none, except in the field, my sorrow spread thin, soft cries heard on the breath of the wind.

THE LAST STOP SANDWICH SHOP

The final bell of the school year rang and the cheers of students could be heard for miles. Papers flung around in a whirlwind of fluttering pages, notebooks filled with doodles and half-hearted notes discarded for the summer. Teenagers erupted from the doors, discussing summer plans: vacations, parties, relaxing by the beach, and for Chelsea, a long, drawn-out, truly miserable summer job.

While other teens fled to their cars and bikes, anxious to beat the encroaching summer heat and start their fun, Chelsea kicked aside pencils and books on the hall floor, meandering out through the doors, unwilling to accept that exiting school wouldn't mean any extra freedom.

"Hey, wait up!" Dan said

"Wait for what?" Chelsea asked. "My life to be over?"

"Oh, come on, Miss Dramatic, it's not that bad. It's just a summer job at a sandwich shop. Short hours, free food, and finally a little extra cash."

"It's a prison!" Chelsea said, flailing her arms in the air. "If I want to go somewhere, I'll have to request time off. What if it's a really good beach day? Or a movie gets an early drop online?"

"You're not going to miss every beach day there ever was, Chels. And with the extra cash, you can actually pay to go to the movies and maybe even buy us a big tub of popcorn. With the refills."

"Ah, yes. You're totally right. I'll just sell my soul for some buttery calories. Problem solved."

The pair finally reached the exit, the heavy metal doors clanging shut behind them.

"And boom goes my freedom," Chelsea said, groaning as the two walked to her car.

Chelsea ducked her brown-haired head into the driver's side, catching a reflection of her tired hazel eyes in the car window. She sighed. Dan settled in next to her, his spiky blond hair—desperately trying to bring back 2000s fashion—nestled under a backwards ball cap.

She turned on the car, cranked the music up as loud as she could, and left the parking lot dreading the days to come.

The next morning, Chelsea stared at herself in the mirror, fighting back disgust. A truly tragic image faced her: black stretch pants, black polo two sizes too large, apron tied overtop. Black visor cap, stray hairs from her ponytail framing her head like a halo.

She sighed, as that seemed to be the only noise she could produce these days. Heading downstairs, giving a quick wave goodbye to her mom, Chelsea felt her chest tighten. The stress of the new job was already taking its toll.

The whole drive to work, Chelsea contemplated shifting the steering wheel hard left to set her on the way to the beach. She resisted the urge, telling herself that maybe it wouldn't be so bad, that having extra cash would be great by the end of summer so she could finally start buying herself the things she wanted instead of waiting for her mom to catch on by Christmas.

Plus, there was all that stuff about personal growth and the value of hard work and yada yada that her mom suggested, proud of her daughter.

Chelsea felt her nervousness grow, and by the time she reached the sandwich shop, at the end of a long drive off the freeway, she felt sick to her stomach. The repetitious thought plagued her mind: *what if I'm bad at making sandwiches?* The only thing worse than the job itself was completely sucking at it.

She parked her car, took a couple of deep breaths, and exited. The broken-down sign flickered above, declaring the name of the restaurant: Last Shop Sandwich Stop.

Chelsea had seen the ad for a "sandwich artist" in the newspaper. No previous experience required, decent enough pay for her first job, flexible hours. She'd called to inquire and was hired on the spot. A few days later, her uniform arrived in a blank cardboard box on her doorstep. Chelsea was pretty sure most jobs didn't work this way, but she wasn't about to complain at how smooth the process had been.

Oh well, she thought. *A job's a job.*

She pushed the door to the restaurant open and was greeted by a sea of the most artificial smiles she'd ever seen. An older gentleman, dressed in all black, rushed forward to greet her.

"You must be Chelsea," he said to her, extending his hand. Chelsea hesitantly took it, and he jerked his arm up and down like an old rusted lever that needed a good greasing. The man beamed at her, flashing bright white teeth.

"That's me," she said, meekly.

"Well, I'm Roger, the manager. Been working here at The Last Stop Sandwich Shop for twenty years now. At the rate I'm going, it probably will be my final stop indeed!"

Chelsea faked a laugh. "Yeah, sure does smell good in here," she said, hoping to move things along.

"We bake our bread fresh. Try to locally source our veggies and meats too. People come from all around for our sandwiches." Chelsea thought that to be strange, seeing as she'd lived in this town her whole life and never heard of this particular sandwich shop.

"Cool. Gotta make sure to try one for lunch then," Chelsea said. Her stomach growled in response at the mention of food.

"Why don't you try one now? What suits your food fancy?" Roger asked.

Chelsea eyed the menu, a simple chalkboard with colorful markings all over it.

"What would you suggest?"

"Hmm," Roger thought aloud. "Perhaps our special of the day! You'll love it if you like fresh sliced deli meats. It's a row of each our finest meats. We call it the 'Meat Your Maker'. One of the best sellers we've got."

"Sure, that sounds good," she said. "Say, where are all the customers?" She gestured around the empty restaurant, where only she, Roger, and three other employees occupied the lobby.

"The lunch rush will come. Sometimes it feels like it swallows us whole." Roger placed his arm around Chelsea's shoulder. "Let's get you settled in the back while Mattie here makes your sandwich." Mattie, a blonde girl with a pixie cut and a cool rainbow pin stuck in her visor, started pulling ingredients from the various stations.

The two walked to the back. The walls were lined with metal racks, holding vegetables, chips, bottled drinks, napkins, and other paper materials needed to run the shop. Chelsea could have sworn she caught the mouth-watering scent of bread baking, but as far as she could tell, there was nothing more to the back room than what was in plain view. The sink was overflowing with dirty dishes. The wall furthest from the entrance had two heavy metal doors, with a smaller door between them.

"The walk-ins. We have a freezer and refrigerator. They don't typically lock behind you, but sometimes the doors get a little stuck with their powerful suctioning. But don't worry, there's an emergency button in there if you're really stuck. Wouldn't want any more people freezing to death in there."

Chelsea raised an eyebrow.

"Kidding, kidding," Roger said, hands in the air. "Though I'm sure Bread Boy would be happy for a frozen snack."

"Bread Boy?" Chelsea asked.

"Don't worry. You probably won't meet him. We only feed the bad employees to him."

Chelsea wasn't sure how to respond, so she kept her mouth shut. Roger nonchalantly continued the tour.

"If you have to use the restroom or you need a good cry, we only have the one bathroom in the lobby. Lockers are over here. Breaks are taken when you need them. Food is fifty percent off."

Only fifty percent? So much for free food, Chelsea thought.

Roger put his hands on his hips, elbows pointed out, smile plastered on his face.

"Here endeth the tour," Roger said. "I'll bet Mattie has your sandwich ready. Eat up. First one's free. Then I'll have the crew show you the ropes on how to make a sandwich. Just shadow them for a bit and I'm sure you'll learn the art of the sandwich in no time."

With that, he disappeared into the back, leaving Chelsea at the front of the store. Mattie appeared, the sandwich she had prepared in a red tray with sheets of paper underneath the food. It was monstrously huge, chunks of meat lined up between cheese and vegetables, sauce spilling over the sides.

"One Meat Your Maker, served with all the best fixings." Mattie handed the sandwich over, and Chelsea's wrist buckled at the weight. "Don't come back until you eat it all. Newcomer ritual."

Chelsea thanked Mattie and headed to a nearby table. She sat, taking in the strange day so far. Taking her first bite of the sandwich, Chelsea prayed that the job would be smooth sailing from here on out.

Smooth sailing it was for the first few weeks Chelsea worked at The Last Stop Sandwich Shop. She learned the sandwich recipes, deep-cleaned the store until her arms felt like Jell-

O, and picked up more than her fair share of olives from the floor beneath tables.

While the shop was empty on her first day, Roger was right about the way a rush could swallow you whole. Some days were slow, but when it rained customers, it poured. It felt like someone was dropping them off by the busload some lunch hours.

Her job was fine as far as low-wage jobs went. She worked hard, knew she should be paid more, but also hoped to get enough experience under her belt to find a new job next summer. She'd even learned to tolerate the strangeness of the shop, to some extent. Though, no matter what she did, Chelsea couldn't figure out where the fresh bread was baked and why she always caught a faint scent of the cooking dough in the back room. She'd investigated, high and low, all except for the square trash chute between the freezer and fridge. There, the scent was the strongest, wrapped with the sour smell of garbage. Chelsea wasn't about to go headfirst down the small passageway, so she shrugged it off and forced her mind to stop wandering.

Chelsea was on a break when she heard it. A low beep that came from the back room, startling her from her daydreaming in front of the tomato slicer. She turned her head slowly, towards the back room, her ears perking to the beeping. Following the repetitive noise, she walked slowly to the back, unsure of what would meet her. The beep grew louder as the walk-in freezer came into view. The emergency buzzer. As she faced the rest of the back wall, Chelsea caught a blur of movement between the two large walk-ins. A *thump* resounded and the hatch of the center door slammed shut.

Her heart beat louder than she would have thought possible, and the world tunneled around her, focusing on the sudden movement. Chelsea stood frozen, startled at whatever had just transpired. Her mind screamed a warning to her, not able to comprehend what could have gone through the chute, the back room empty.

Her surroundings came back into clarity around her, the beeping reminding her of why she'd come to the back room. She made her way to the freezer briskly and flung the door open as fast as she could despite the suction.

Mattie was inside, shivering.

"Oh, thank God!" Mattie said.

"You okay? What happened?" Chelsea asked.

"I was getting some meat to put in the fridge to thaw and someone came in after me. Whatever it was, it bit my leg, left, then held the door shut."

"That's... unnerving," Chelsea said. "Is your leg okay?"

"Yeah, I think so. It didn't pierce the skin, but I didn't get a good look at whatever did it."

"We should find Roger," Chelsea suggested.

The two walked out of the freezer and jumped back slightly when they opened the door, Roger standing before them.

"You scared the crap out of me," Chelsea said.

"Sorry, I just thought I heard a commotion. Everything okay?" Roger said.

"Something attacked Mattie!" Chelsea blurted.

Roger's face flushed with anger. "I swear if that Bread Boy stepped out of line... I'll have to have a word with him."

"Is Bread Boy your dog? Or some kind of animal? I saw something go flying down the trash chute when I came into the back," Chelsea said. This was the second mention of him since she'd started the job. But she still hadn't heard anything more than his name.

Roger waved her off. "Not to bother. I'm going to go have a talk with him." He walked away, headed out the back door.

"Who's the Bread Boy?" Chelsea asked.

Mattie's face turned into a frown. "Just a stupid joke Roger always makes. 'Better not upset the Bread Boy, so don't throw away food. The Bread Boy hates when you over-toast sandwiches.' He's not real. I don't think."

Chelsea was perplexed. *What an odd way to motivate your employees.*

Mattie grabbed Chelsea's arm and hauled her out to the lobby. "We better take care of these customers," Mattie said, adjusting her visor so it sat neatly on her hair. Like magic, a line of hungry people had formed, nearly wrapped around back to the front door.

"What about your leg?"

"It's fine. Whatever it was, it didn't break the skin. I probably just imagined it. Just a charley horse or something."

Chelsea sighed, certain she was losing her mind. She was concerned about Mattie, a sense of kinship having grown between them during their time in the great sandwich shop trenches together. *I'll keep an eye on her, make sure she's okay*, Chelsea though, putting on a pair of thin plastic gloves and taking out her bread knife. *Time to get to work.*

The next day, Roger was waiting for Chelsea as she made her way back to the sandwich shop.

"Morning, boss," Chelsea said.

"Have you been throwing away scrap food in the trash?" Roger asked, starting right in, an annoyed look on his face.

Chelsea didn't know how to respond. Where else was garbage supposed to go? They couldn't use the tiny excess bread, or bruised vegetables or meat that had gone past their expiry date. "Yes?" she answered, a question at the edge of voice.

"Did no one tell you that food goes down that chute in the back?"

"That little square between the two walk-ins?"

"The one and only," Roger replied, frustration still evident in his voice.

Chelsea tried to recollect if anyone had mentioned that. "I don't think anyone did, but I could be mistaken. I'm sorry, I'll make sure to save it for the chute next time."

"Have you ever seen any of the other employees throwing food away?" Come to think of it, she hadn't.

"No. Look, I'm really sorry, I didn't know and I didn't realize."

Roger put his finger in the air, as if to make his point clearer. "Nothing is wasted here. *Nothing*. Not food. Not time."

"Got it. I'll do better," Chelsea said. "Scout's honor."

"All right. The Last Stop Sandwich Shop appreciates you. Let's make this a good day, okay?"

Chelsea turned the odd start of the day around, making sure to gather the food that would have gone into the trash into a tiny bag. When there was a lull in the line of customers, she took the bag to the back room and stood in front of the chute. It was about two and half feet tall and three feet wide. She opened the chute, the door swinging downwards. At first, she caught the scent of fresh baked bread once again, until she was met with a blast of fetid air, like rotten food. The smell was disgusting, so she quickly placed the food on the small ramp and sent it sliding below.

The rest of the week went without incident. With no further weird Roger lectures, Chelsea was feeling quite hopeful about her place at the shop. She and Mattie had started the kindling of a friendship, vowing to hang out on their next shared shift off.

On the morning of her next shift, Chelsea's phone buzzed. It was Dan. Probably calling her to invite her to yet another beach party she couldn't go to.

"Hey, Dan," she said, answering her phone.

"What's up, Chels? Please tell me you aren't working tonight."

"I shouldn't be. What're you thinking?"

"There's a slasher movie double feature. Want to go? My treat."

Chelsea beamed. "What, you don't want me to spend my hard-earned cash?" she joked.

"You can get the popcorn."

"Deal. See you tonight?"

Dan cheered over the phone. "You bet. I'll send you the time. Later, dork."

Chelsea hung up her phone, already excited to get the day's work over with.

Within thirty minutes, she was at the shop. When she got there, though, there was an air of something strange in the workplace. Everyone seemed rushed. Roger burst forward from the back, accosting Chelsea immediately.

"Chelsea, I need you to work a double today. Mattie was supposed to do it but she called in sick."

"Sick? I hope she's okay," Chelsea responded, worried about her new friend. "I don't know if I can… I made plans for the night."

"Please, Chelsea, I'm begging you. You'll get overtime."

Chelsea contemplated her options. She didn't owe him anything, and the movies would be really fun, but if she wanted a good recommendation from this place she thought it best to keep the boss happy. But… this job had already taken so much of her time.

"Sorry, Roger," she replied. "I already have tickets for an event tonight."

"Please," Roger said, hands pressed together, pleading with her.

"I'm sorry, I really can't," she said resolutely.

"Fine. That's really too bad for us all," Roger said, before storming off.

Chelsea shrugged internally, happy for standing her ground. She clocked in and got ready to spend the day making sandwiches.

The day went fast, but Chelsea was beat by the end of her shift. She just had a few more things to do before she left for the day. She had been gathering food scraps, carefully following Roger's strict food disposal directions.

She was standing next to the chute, about to reach in, when she heard the emergency buzzer go off next to her head. Startled, she jumped an inch in the air, her heart racing.

Chelsea faced the freezer, the buzzing incessant. Her mind was spinning, wondering who could be stuck in there. All the other employees were out front.

Steeling herself, she swung open the door, but was mystified by what she saw. Nothing. There was nothing in there but a chill in the air.

Out of nowhere, Chelsea felt arms encircle her waist, though she could see nothing grabbing her. The force pushed her out of the walk-in, grabbed her again, and slammed her against the chute, disorienting her.

Chelsea fell to the floor, looking around in a panicked state. She couldn't see her assailant anywhere.

The next thing she knew, the chute flew open, and she heard a soft thump inside the metal tunnel. Before she could do anything else, a cold hand encircled her wrist and pulled her through the opening of the chute.

Down she tumbled, into the darkness of whatever was at the end of the passageway. She landed in a heap at the bottom, still gripping the bag of excess food she had meant to toss in the chute before she was attacked.

It was pitch black in the room, and it reeked like years of rotten food and spoiled milk. Chelsea couldn't help but think that it smelled like the living dead had taken up residence in the dank room.

Chelsea felt around the floor, trying to find a wall or something to cling to and fight with. Her hands encircled something cloth, with a hard rim. *A visor*, she thought. Just like the one on her head. Except, this one had a tiny rainbow pin stuck in the top. *Oh no...* she thought, *Mattie. How did this get down there?*

Chelsea continued to stumble around, and soon her question was answered when she tripped over a prone leg. She'd found Mattie. Or at least part of her.

Her eyes began adjusting to the dark, though she could still barely see much in front of her. Before she could process what was happening, she felt hot, wet, and heavy breathing in her ear. She turned to face the sound, and could barely make out a hunkering form, green and scaly with tufts of fur on its body. She'd never seen anything like it before.

It was slimy and dirty, and blood rimmed its mouth. *Mattie's blood*, Chelsea thought. *I have to get out of here!*

She turned and ran back to where she thought the chute was, trying to make her way up the smooth metal surface. She screamed.

"Help! Help!"

The monster was right on her heels, growling under its breath.

"Please, somebody!"

She made it a few feet up the chute before she felt a clawed hand around her ankle. She turned to kick it off and screamed at its ghastly appearance, warts covering the skin.

The door to the chute opened above, casting light down the tunnel and onto Chelsea. She could still feel the hand around her ankle, but in the light, it turned invisible.

Despite the fact that it had disappeared from sight, the grip on her leg continued, the fingers digging in and rubbing her flesh raw.

A voice called out from above.

"Chelsea? Are you down there?"

"Oh, thank God, Roger. Help! There's a monster down here."

"Ah. I see you've met Bread Boy."

Chelsea was so confused, she stopped struggling for a second. Roger continued talking above her.

"One of our best employees. Takes care of all the garbage around here."

"He's a monster! He ate Mattie!"

Roger chuckled above. "Now that's not very nice. He's a great worker and really bakes the best bread. But Mattie… she messed up on a few too many orders today. And, well… just like the trash. Disposable."

"You'll be arrested! Someone will come looking for her. Someone will come looking for me!" Chelsea screamed and began thrashing with all her might.

"Runaways, the both of you. Believable in this small town."

Chelsea felt hopeless inside. She was running out of energy, but the tugging at her leg continued.

"Please," Chelsea said, trying one more time. "Please help me."

Roger clucked his tongue at her. "You should have taken the overtime. We waste nothing here. I told you that before."

Chelsea's heart dropped. With one huge tug the monster yanked her from the chute. It was once again bathed in darkness, and Chelsea could see its disgusting form hulking over her.

"We here at The Last Stop Sandwich Shop thank you for your service." The metallic clank rang above as Roger shut the door to the chute.

Chelsea screamed one last time as the monster lurched forward, licking its lips.

Dinner time.

GREEN THUMBS STILL BLEED RED

When Faye saw the girl from across the swap meet walkway, she knew she had to meet her. The girl was captivating in her overalls, her arm full of succulents overflowing from the bent crooks of her elbows; absolutely radiant. The sun spilled behind her, filtering through her dark brown curls, reflecting onto her freckled face.

The plants bundled in the girl's arms began to wobble, and Faye saw her chance. She put the antique camera she had contemplated purchasing back down on the table, gathered her courage, and rushed forward to the meet the girl.

"Whoa, whoa!" the girl said as one of the succulents tumbled from her arm.

Faye reached over, grabbed the plant midair, thankful that her clumsy hands actually worked for a change. She cradled the odd-looking plant, something long, tubular, green and fuchsia. It was curved at the tip, bulbous and hollow. Faye pondered how she'd never really seen anything quite like it.

"Oh jeez, thank you," the girl said, readjusting the remaining bundle of plants in her arms. "I just got so excited seeing all these little guys that I really did myself dirty."

The girl walked towards the table with the cash box, ready to purchase her items. She smiled, her off-kilter grin melting Faye's heart.

"Let me just…" she said, placing the items down on the table. She offered her hand to Faye. "There. I'm Jackie."

Faye took her hand, feeling her heart thunder as the warmth of Jackie's hand enveloped hers and diffused up her arm. "Faye. Pleasure to meet you. I was uh… happy to provide the assist back there."

The two held each other's gaze, heat flowing into their cheeks. Faye felt a sharp sting on her arm, dropping her eyes to the offending area.

"Ow! Dammit," she said, rubbing the sore spot. She hadn't seen anything fly or jump off, but the skin that had pressed against the plant she had held was burning. She placed the plant on the table with the others and examined her arm, finding a small spot puckered and red.

"You okay?" Jackie asked, rushing forward.

"Yeah, must have been a bee or something."

"Let me see," Jackie said. She held Faye's arm near the red spot. "Looks like it. Skin's a little strangely contoured though."

Faye sighed. Just her luck.

"Well, I should probably take my strangely contoured skin back on home soon. It's getting hot out here."

Jackie nodded. "Summer's hitting hard. Thank you again for saving my little plant."

"No problem. You've got quite a variety there. I've never seen anything like this guy."

"The one you grabbed is called *Darlingtonia californica*, or the cobra plant. I've been looking for one of these forever! I have the perfect pot for it."

Faye admired the way Jackie's face lit up talking about the plants. If there was one thing Faye enjoyed, it was seeing people talk about the things they loved.

"Are you like a real-life Poison Ivy or something?"

"…or something." Jackie grinned. "I've got a wild collection at home. I know this is awfully forward, but I'd really love to show you my plant babies, if you'd be up for it. I don't live too far from here. Walking distance."

Faye rubbed her still-throbbing arm and contemplated her options. Something in her gut told her this wasn't the kind of girl she wanted to let go.

"Sure. I'd be happy to. Maybe get a little disinfectant on whatever is going on here," she said, pointing to her red skin.

Jackie beamed and turned to the plant vendor, who had been silently watching the exchange between the two women. She paid the man, who then helped her to package her new plants.

"Here, let me help you with that," Faye said, grabbing a box of her purchases.

Jackie blushed. "I already don't know what I'd do without you."

The pair walked the short distance to a high-rise apartment complex down the street. Upon entering Jackie's home, Faye was almost immediately overwhelmed by the amount of green in the space. It was beautiful and intimidating, like a slice of an exotic jungle feeling almost misplaced between the stark white walls of the cramped space.

"Wow. This is really something," Faye said, taking it all in.

"I've been collecting and growing plants for years. My favorite little hobby." Jackie placed the plants on her dining room table.

"I'm sure these new ones will fit right in," Faye said.

Jackie looked deep into Faye's eyes. "Certainly not the only thing that seems to."

Faye's heart swelled, and the rest was history.

From the corner of the room the cobra plant squirmed.

Faye and Jackie enjoyed their budding romance over the next six months. They spent their weekends looking for vintage cameras for Faye and new plants for Jackie's collection. The two truly had a symbiotic relationship. Jackie was able to showcase her infamous plants thanks to Faye's capable eye behind the camera, and Faye was the happiest she'd ever been in a relationship.

But in the same way that their journey together started, it was fated to end: by the handing off of an exotic plant.

The two had exchanged "I love you"s several weeks earlier, but the fire of the romance felt like it was dying already, at least to Faye and her previously broken heart. She was protective of her love, having shared it too often before only to get burned. So she took her time with Jackie. But Jackie... Jackie had chiseled away at the chains holding Faye's heart. Had found that seed within and nurtured it, like the plants she was so good with.

Faye was already afraid to lose it. Afraid she'd wither under her own black thumb.

On their anniversary, the two were sharing a candlelit dinner in Jackie's apartment. The plants loomed around them, casting dancing shadows of vines and leaves on the walls by the flickering light.

"To a beautiful year together," Jackie said, raising her glass of wine.

"And hopefully more," Faye said, clinking her pint glass with her girlfriend's.

"I have something for you," Jackie said, reaching beside the table.

Faye's heart thudded as Jackie placed the cobra plant, wrapped in a ribbon, onto the top of the table. It had grown considerably in size since she'd seen it last, having blended in with the other foliage in the apartment.

The plant was thriving.

Faye's initial emotional response of gratitude was quickly overwhelmed by the responsibility of having to take care of the plant. She remembered how Jackie had told her it was a bog plant, usually populating the Pacific Northwest.

"Just feed it some bugs. Crickets or something dead. It'll probably also catch some of the pests around your place too."

"Look, I don't know—"

"Ice-cold water, a humid-ish climate, and it should be just fine."

"I'm not sure I'll be able to…" Faye trailed off, looking at the overjoyed expression on her girlfriend's face. "Okay. I'll try. Anything for you." She puffed her chest, raised her voice to sound like an old pulp hero. "I'll keep this plant alive, or by God I'll die trying."

And try she did. She watered the plant daily, humming to it, urging it to grow. As her relationship with Jackie continued a downhill spiral, Faye felt her relationship with the plant growing. It became a symbol of their love, and Faye wanted so badly to keep it very much alive.

The cobra plant began to wilt, the tubular portions breaking down, growing soft, caving in on itself. The new walls Faye had so carefully constructed around her heart, sturdy, but with doors for Jackie to come and go from, and windows for the world to see it beat, began to crumble too.

Faye hung her head by the plant, her defeat overtaking her. The monotony of the relationship, the love replaced with complacency, the tunnel closing on the last train out. And she couldn't even keep this stupid plant alive.

Her hands gripped the sides of the table, thinking about how Jackie had become increasingly tied up at work, tied up with social outings, tied up with parts of her life that she opted not to share with Faye.

Faye's anger simmered at Jackie, who barely had time for her girlfriend, seemed flippant when Faye tried to talk things through with her. Her anger simmered so, but when Faye thought about her own culpability in letting the relationship die because it was easier than fighting for it she didn't just simmer—she violently boiled.

Her head dipped towards the cobra plant, her blood roiling. She felt the bite. She slapped her hand to her forehead above her right eyebrow, feeling a sharp sting and a quick puckering of the skin.

It had drawn blood.

Her gaze darted around her apartment, looking for the offending bee or mosquito or whatever had bit or stung her.

She saw and heard nothing. Until she looked down, at her smiling cobra plant.

A splash of red dotted its uppermost tube, a drop of blood inching its way down the hollow structure.

As the blood made its way through the plant, the course outer layer of the dying flora became smooth and radiant again.

It bit me. And it liked it. Faye's mind was racing, wondering if something was wrong with the plant. If it was defective. If *she* was defective.

She remembered the first time she'd met Jackie—and this very cobra plant for that matter—at the swap meet. She had cradled this plant in her arms after Jackie had nearly dropped it. She'd felt that sting on her arm, and her skin had adorned that strange abrasion afterwards.

She shuffled off to the bathroom, leaned forward in the mirror and examined the spot above her eyebrow. A red, angry welt looked back at her, marred by the same unique contour her arm had suffered before.

The cobra plant had struck her then, and it struck her now as well.

Was it stressed? Did I stress it out and it lashed out at me in return?

Faye went back to the patio to examine the plant. It looked normal: a whole lot healthier than it had a few minutes prior to her bloodletting. She half expected it to break into song like Jackie's favorite musical. It didn't.

Faye paced in front of the plant. *I helped it. Brought it back to life. It just needed a piece of me.*

Faye thought about calling Jackie, confident that she'd be thrilled with her findings. She forced it down, not wanting to bother her girlfriend at work. She kept it inside, bottled up.

And so it went.

The relationship grew more distant, so much so that Faye barely heard from Jackie some days. Jackie swore up and down when they saw each other that she was still in it. That she still wanted Faye, that they were meant to be together, but she was just *so damn busy* all the time. But to Faye, who'd heard it before, they were just words.

The plant withered. Faye watched it, bitterly, fuming at it silently for wanting to die under her care. No amount of water or plant food or insects seemed to keep it alive. It only seemed to want her. Unlike her relationship—which was dying under her watch, in tandem with the plant—but which she herself could not cure.

Another text. A withered plant. A thumb-prick of blood. Resurgence.

Another broken date. A plant wilted to the floor. A thimbleful of red liquid down its tube. Growth.

She watched the plant from the corner of her eye as she walked past it, the red-green coloring a blur in her vision. Its stems would bend in her direction, following her as if magnetized to her presence, haunting her movement. It wanted blood. It was *all* it wanted. But it was no hunter.

Her phone buzzed. A text from Jackie. *Gotta cancel dinner tonight. Sorry.*

Faye's anger mounted. She tried to call. Once. Twice. No answer.

A message. "Again, Jackie? The third time this week? You know what, it's over. Come get your stupid plant. We're done."

She'd given her everything she had to make this work. It had, for a while, but it wasn't enough. Unsustainable. So, it was done. Everything she had, but none of it was needed.

The plant followed her pacing, the tubes shifting back and forth as she walked a rut into the hardwood.

Her eyes fell in line with the plant, tracing her steps. Eyes vacillating back and forth like a metronome, she watched the plant. She felt it, pulling her close.

Faye approached the plant. She looked at her finger, then at the plant's pocked epidermis. It was dying, and she could save it.

She shook her hand, heard her fingers flapping as it jolted around before she let it dangle towards the floor, letting the blood flow to it.

Holding her hand out to the plant, she waited for it to strike. It snapped forward, its tubes circling her finger, sucking.

The sharp sting of its snare almost made Faye jerk her hand away, but she held it aloft, and the plant continued to imbibe. The red liquid flowed freely down the hatch of the plant, who all but gulped her down its throat. The tube moved further up her finger, taking more of it in its mouth until it was past her second joint.

Faye couldn't believe how healthy the plant looked, positively thriving with the bloodbath it was relishing in internally.

Is it growing? Ever so slightly, she decided.

Faye felt herself growing weak as the plant continued to sip the blood from her veins. A calmness overtook her as she felt the thick hairs inside the plant's gullet taking her finger in further. She gave a gentle tug back, but it wouldn't let go, and the motion only served to send her deeper.

A second finger. A third. Her thumb. Her palm.

It sank within the plant, who was full-throated with her hand up to her wrist.

The blood flowed more freely than before, the vein punctured by the plant who continued to eat.

A human IV.

Faye closed her eyes, accepting the darkness that folded around her.

The plant continued to drink.

And it would until there was nothing left for it.

Nothing left that Faye could give to the relationship that wanted it all.

Five days later, the apartment door opened. Jackie stepped in, calling Faye's name. She had finally gotten a chance to come over after hearing Faye's message. Had gathered the courage to try and work things out.

She knew it was late, but she hoped it was better late than never.

Her heart hammered as she inspected the apartment, looking for any sign of where Faye might be. She rounded the corner, Faye's name on her lips, and she found her.

Jackie screamed, horrified, in disbelief.

Faye lay on the floor, her arm hanging in the air. Her hand was engulfed by the cobra plant up to her wrist, the plant three times the size it was before. Thriving.

Unlike its host, Faye, who was all but desiccated on the ground, her skin a dry, pallid gray, withered. Her face pinched together, as if having sucked a lemon dry, wrinkles invading her face.

Faye had kept her promise to Jackie. The plant was very much so alive, and Faye had died trying.

MR. GIGGLES

Alice cheered when her mom said it was time to go to the dentist. She watched her mom's face turn into a confused smile, unable to understand the excitement Alice felt. Who could blame her? Sitting in the stuffy office, while she waited for her six-year-old to get prodded with bluntly sharp instruments by the strange man obsessed enough with mouths to make it his career, hardly seemed like a fun day.

But Alice beamed, ready to make the fifteen-minute drive to the dentist, the thought of her teeth being scraped distant compared to her joy and readiness to see her friend. By the time they reached the building, Alice all but bolted from the car and into the office. Her mom called out for her to stop, but opted to jog lightly behind her to keep up because there was no stopping the bundle of energy.

Alice burst through the doors, zeroed in on her target: the small arcade room off the orthodontist wing. This dentist had figured out just how to make kids cooperative. Place a few video games at every part of the visit, and kids would barely realize they were being tortured in the name of tooth health. It was paradise: the arcade room in the waiting room, the consoles once inside, one for each chair with a television set hanging from the ceiling within sight of the patients.

One game stood above the rest for Alice, and that was the simulated racecar driving arcade cabinet. She loved sitting in the seat, turning the sticky wheel right and left on the track. Alice wouldn't learn to drive for years to come, but she loved feeling like she was actually controlling the whirring car along the graphical track. The arcade cabinet was old, too dated for most of the kids who visited the office, but Alice could never get enough. The dental assistant would all but have to drag her out of the seat when it was her turn for her teeth cleaning.

Alice's mom couldn't figure it out. Her tiny daughter was never as transfixed as she was making that drive through the virtual race. She came in last each time, as her hand-eye coordination wasn't especially finetuned quite yet, driving slowly through the grass rather than on the circular track. How she got the car to move at all confused her mom, as there were no physics possible that meant her daughter's stubby child legs could reach the pedals. But the pedals were boxed in, so her mom couldn't quite see what was happening.

She clicked her tongue, shook her head and smiled. Her daughter was happy and that was all that mattered. She went to sit just outside the room to wait for Alice's name to be called for her six-month mouth prods.

Alice slammed her little fists on the worn rubber wheel at the race's end. She was having a blast, but she was getting sick of losing. Before starting the next race, Alice peered into the opening near her feet, the boxed enclosure of the pedals just in sight.

"Mr. Giggles? You really need to stop laying on the slow down pedal so much."

The tiny imp glared up at her, raising its clawed fist. "C'mon kid, whaddya expect? You're the eyes, I'm the feets. You can't win without me."

"I can't win *with* you," she muttered under her breath.

"Okay, okay," he put both hands up, surrendering. "I'll cut you a deal. You win the next race, and I'll grant you one wish."

"Anything?" Alice asked, eyes wide.

"Anything."

Alice tucked her head to her chest, in her thinking pose, weighing her options. "And if I can't win?"

The imp looked devilishly back at her. "I'll still grant you the wish, but you may not want it."

"Okay," Alice replied. She hopped back on the seat. "Let's do this."

The race started; Alice lost.

She got back down on her hands and knees and looked for her friend in the black void of the pedal box. "Mr. Giggles? Can I still have my wish?"

"Sure, kid. But like I said, you may not want it."

"I want it," she said, determined. "I wish I could play this game forever and never have to see the dentist after."

"I can see you've got a lot goin' on between those ears, kid. All right, wish granted."

At the ripe age of six, Alice clutched her chest as spasms wracked her body. She fell to the ground, still for only a moment before the screams started. Her mom had heard the thump and turned to the room, shrieking about her baby, dead. Everyone panicked, calling emergency services, clutching other tiny children to them close, hoping the heart attack wasn't contagious. Everyone, so caught up in the death of Alice, sweet Alice, that they didn't notice the arcade cabinet booting up a race.

No one could see the little girl's ghost, tongue between her teeth in concentration, extending her ghostly legs to reach the pedals, finally winning the race.

Mr. Giggles slunk out of the arcade, freed from his hole, and ready to take up residence in another arcade machine, lying in wait to grant the wish of the next eager child.

The dentist, it turns out, really is quite hellish.

Part Two: To Break

REPLENISH

Like all good pyramid schemes, it sounds too good to be true. Your friend, who you haven't seen in person for over three years, appears suddenly on your doorstep, bag of cosmetics in hand, swearing her life on some kind of make-up. An all-in-one anti-aging, anti-acne, barely-notice-it's-there miracle cream.

"Apply it once a day, every day. Results immediately!" your friend squeaks out excitedly.

"How much?" you ask.

"That's the best part! The cost is so low per bottle. Makes it easy to keep up with the routine and never run out." She winks. It's as if she knows your weakness. That you've spent more time staring at your wrinkly, old face in the mirror than you care to admit. That you've pounded your fist into the countertop, again and again, as the years have passed and your face, your success, your *legacy* succumbed to the aging process.

"You have the make-up on now?" you ask, studying your friend's face.

"I do! Every day, without fail. It's not make-up, though. We call it more of a see-through face. Adding color, vibrancy, *life*." The last word drips from her lips, plump and young.

You contemplate her face, noting that it does, in fact, look silky smooth, dynamic almost, lowlights and highlights in all the right places in the most effortless way. Natural, beautiful. *Young.*

She sees your careful consideration, continues her spiel. "With this cream, you can keep your face on forever." You can't help but to feel a bit of a sinister undertone in her words, a quiet plea in her voice.

"When in Rome, or something like that," you reply, smiling kindly, after a thoughtful moment. You remember seeing on social media something about your friend's divorce and lost job. You figure you can kill a couple of birds with a single wad of cash, doing a kind thing for a sort-of friend and maybe making your own life a little better in the process.

She thanks you, urging you to call if you need new stock once the bottle runs out. Promises that you'll see results within an hour and never look another year older.

You walk inside, smiling at your purchase. At this point in your life, pyramid scheme or not, you'd give almost anything a try.

The next morning you study your face in the bathroom mirror. A pale complexion, marred by sun and oil and lines from—God forbid—too much smiling looks back at you. Two eyes, bags underneath, dart around, taking in every mark, line, and discoloring the reflection has to offer. You've long grown weary of watching your face age by the minute, watching divots appear as if by magic overnight, certain there's been some monster in the dark scratching scars into your skin. But no, no monsters, just the passage of time.

Like the call of a siren, the idea of reversing a downward slope into looking your age is tantalizing. You know all the platitudes about beauty being on the inside, looking "respectable" not "old", and feeling guilted into accepting and owning your physical wisdom and experience, worn on your face.

But wouldn't it just be *nice*…

Nice to look good and not just good for your age.

You investigate the bottle of cream. The label is sparse, no list of ingredients or name. Just a simple "Apply once per day, every day, consistently" written in black letters around the bottom of the bottle.

The design choice, lack of marketing and snazzy colors takes you aback for a moment. You almost set the bottle down. Instead, you steal one last look at your wrinkled, worn face, mumble a quick "Screw it," and open the lid. You submerge the tips of your fingers in its thick contents.

The cream goes on like frosting under a knife. It's instantly cool to the touch, providing the snappy feeling of exfoliation without the abrasiveness. You become mesmerized as you swirl the buttery cream over your face, in the crease of your nose, between your eyebrows, taking careful time in the corners of your eyes where the crow's feet have landed.

Beautiful. You look beautiful.

Just like you did on your daily news segments, at the peak of your stardom. Just like you did during the height of your pregnancy, glowing skin radiating the beauty growing within. Just like you did at your second wedding, before your daughter graduated, left for school. Just like you did when you had it all.

You nearly weep at the results. In moments, your face looks nothing like it once had, back a few minutes ago when you had nothing but a bottle full of hope. You are no longer the ex-newscaster, doomed to only write the notes, aged in your wisdom. You are no longer the mother, face worn with worry lines, wondering if your child is surviving at school, flashing those white teeth you envy so, blushing with a smooth face at partners and friends.

You're just you. All you are. The prettiest of faces once again.

The instructions are simple. Apply each day. Every day. And you have obeyed—the results commented on by passersby, stopping because they recognize you, they think, but from some time ago and they just can't quite place it. It feels incredible to be recognized for you, your face, the most important part of you shining on the outside.

But today—today you decide to start the summer differently. You want deeply to neglect your morning routine, no matter how short it is. So, you do.

All day, you lounge on the couch, your face clear of products for the first time in a month. And it feels great. Until—

Your face itches. It shouldn't. It is completely naked and free. But somehow, it feels heavier than ever.

You scratch your face, lightly, but that doesn't stop the chunk of skin from detaching from your cheek, the mass of it filling your nail with a slimy weight. Blood flows from your face, the gouge deep.

"Jesus Christ!" you yell, hopping up and heading towards the bathroom. In the mirror, you take in not only the rugged valley you've carved into your skin, but the cracked mosaic of your face. You can hardly believe it's your own that looks back to you, your skin puckered and torn like a ragged piece of Styrofoam dipped in glue.

Your hands go to the medicine cabinet, past the bandages and disinfectant, and straight for your bottle of cream, which you open and smooth over your face, the thick liquid mingling with blood. Almost instantly, the cracks in your face seal themselves and the throbbing pain lessens.

You don't miss a day of application for the next month.

By the time two months have passed, you're nearly out of the cream.

You frantically try to find the friend from whom you purchased the product on social media, but she has vanished. You don't have her number. You search her name on the internet, hoping to find her, track her down and demand a refreshed stock. Her name in the search bar, you hit enter, and nearly gasp at the results. Local news entries describing a grisly scene. A woman a victim of some kind of acid attack, dead in her home in her bathroom. No suspects, just the death of another beautiful young woman at the hands of some psychopathic intruder.

You know better. Know that she was peddling cursed wares. That her need to feel beautiful outweighed everything else, so she traded her life to a jar full of cream. You know what she did, because now you're stuck in it too.

In just a few days, your own face will melt, slough to the floor, no beauty in death or dignity in your life.

You run to the bathroom, pull the jar from the cabinet. You pore over the label, willing words to appear that simply aren't there. No matter how hard you stare, there's still no product name, no way to replenish your supply.

You weep.

You sob so loud you barely hear your phone ringing over your despair. You jump to your feet, run back to the kitchen where your phone has lit itself up, an unknown number plastered across the screen.

You answer.

The voice on the other end talks slowly, clearly. "We have what you need. You'll find one bottle on your doorstep."

You try to stay calm, but the shaking in your voice betrays you. "And if I need more? How can I reach you?"

"For every person you sell to, we'll give you another three month's supply. Sell this bottle, two more will take its place. One for you, and one for the next set of months."

"And if I don't?" you ask, but you know the answer.

"You'll die as you lived, shallow, broken, and old."

"Damn you," is all you can muster before hanging up the phone.

You walk to your door, open it and try not to jump in surprise at the arrival of the fresh jar of cream, sitting on your doormat like a bar of gold ready for the taking. You snatch it up, hold it close to your chest.

The hammering of your heart wounds you inside, each beat reminding you that you are now a predator and you have to find your prey. You don't want to subject someone else to a life of endless vulnerability, but you also don't want to die.

You want to stay beautiful. You remind yourself it's all you have left.

Running down the list of people you could pawn the scheme to, you realize how few people you know, and how even the ones that you do you didn't deserve this what you'd bring to them.

Old co-anchors? Just as vain as you, but practically inaccessible. The few that had quit the business had families, had made something of themselves once the camera turned off. You can't bear to bring that burden into another circle of people who had done more with their lives than you had managed under the same circumstances.

And family of your own…

Your daughter is too young, too pretty to have need for the cream just yet. And even if she did, her life is full of happiness and love. You're certain at the end of the day, she'd be fine with a face aged by time, knowing that each wrinkle represents the best times of her life.

And your mother, well, she's already doomed to a life of loss of self. Resting in a chair, spending a majority of the day on her back on a nursing room bed, no recollection of herself or you. Her mind is just as wrinkled as her face. You think to yourself that maybe that's the solution. Make yourself forget the rest, don't even stop to recognize the pain of dying.

You chide yourself for even thinking family was an option. You really are as ugly all the way through.

Your decision made, you go back to the bathroom, bottle in hand. Untwisting the cap, you pour. Not into your palms, but into the toilet, flushing immediately. You watch it swirl, around and around, the miracle cream hypnotizing you into thinking you made the wrong decision.

You know you didn't. You finally feel the worm of something your gut. The feeling of doing something that you can finally be proud of, that feels uniquely *you* filling you up.

You'll take that triumph, knowing the pain will come soon. You won't say goodbye. Your family only knows the empty you and it will be easier on them this way.

On the last day of your supply, you drink, miserably, alone on your couch, wondering what will become of your face. What it will feel like despite your best efforts to numb it all away.

The next morning, you learn.

You awake with an itch that turns into a fire. You dare not look in the mirror at what feels like thousands of red ants biting your face. You know there are no insects, only the sharp stings of your face eating itself alive.

Your hands go to your eye sockets, then pull downwards over your cheeks. The flesh comes off in chunks, leaving behind a sticky, red mess.

Your forehead sloughs off on its own, draping down what is left of the bottom half of your face. Finally, your chin falls into your lap.

As you prod the muscles of your face, melting away under your touch, you curse the planned obsolescence of the cream.

Faceless, but finally ageless, you slump.

NEXT DAY DELIVERY

I should have bought a bigger box. My ass has been long asleep, and I've got no more than three inches on any side to move. The Santa costume was a bad idea too. Lots of cushioning, sure, but taking up valuable space in my cardboard prison.

It'll be worth it, though. I can't wait to see the look on her face, the shock, then the pain when I burst from the box and slash her up good. I'll get her boy, too, if the snot-kid is around. I hope he's around.

I can see it all now, playing through my head. The pitch black inside the box and the silence as I sit in the warehouse before the final leg of my trip make it easy to watch it all in my mind. A little projector playing my future sins.

The brown truck will pull up to her new house. Lori's been there for years now, settled in with her new husband and her new baby and her new breasts. The truck driver will heft me out of the back of the vehicle and wheel me up the driveway on his bright red dolly. The box is large, made for furniture, marked "fragile" in bright red letters, and heavy. It is holding a 180-pound man, after all, in what feels like a 300-pound Santa suit and a beard made from the world's itchiest cotton.

The delivery man will park me on the porch, ring the doorbell. My ex-wife will answer, and the postman, unable to resist, will stare at her breasts as he pulls out his clipboard. "Signature, ma'am?" he'll stutter. She'll ask who it's from, and he'll tell her it's from Ted, and she'll squeal that her husband sent her something so large for a Christmas surprise because his typical package is unusually small.

She'll sign for the box, bat her eyes at the delivery man to help her get it inside the house, I'll cross the threshold, and I'll be alone with her for the first time in years (unless the snot-kid is there). I'll wait for the truck to leave, signaled by the sound of the air compressing through the vehicle, and off he'll go and out I'll come.

I'll spring from the box, a red blur with a glint in my eyes and a glint off my knife and that glint will move lightning fast to Lori's face as I *slash slash slash* and make her red like the ornaments on her Christmas tree. Her kid might come down the stairs, so while she's screaming I'll advance on him and tear his arm off first and then hit him about the head with it before moving to his legs. He'll make a great tree topper.

I'll turn my attention back to her, and she's busy trying to put her lip back on her face, goopy liquid dripping through the cleaved open nostril to run down the side of her cheek. I'll take great care to dismember her slowly, intentionally— I want her new husband to see her in her most beautiful state to date.

She'll die. I'll run. I'll enjoy the freedom of having her out of my life in a way that *I* intended.

The plan is perfect. It's run smoothly so far. The delivery driver picked me up on schedule, prepaid shipping, next day delivery. I reckon that about twelve hours have passed. I've slept through most of the drive. I've been at this warehouse for a while now, and I hope to be loaded onto the next truck out of here soon.

All I have to do is wait. Wait in this godforsaken box.

God, this beard really itches.

"This the one?" Krehlborn asks, puffing his cigarette, the white stick dangling out of his mouth.

"Yeah, the postal warehouse for undeliverable packages for this zip code. List says we've got a few in here," Callum responds.

The two elves walk in, the door eclipsing their stature. Their pointed ears and knit caps cast long shadows on the building wall. One of the shadows scratches its ass.

"What are we looking at? Sleigh's already pretty full." Krehlborn examines the piles of packages in disarray, shipping labels destroyed, cardboard caved in.

Callum flicks his finger across the smooth tablet surface. "Says we got one for Sarah from a Tawny. Should be small, probably just a stupid phone case or something."

Krehlborn scans the warehouse, spots his target. "Got it. That was easy. Yep, feels like a phone case. Creative."

The two elves continue, Callum with one hand on the tablet, the other picking some earwax out of his ear.

"How'd you get on this duty anyway?" Callum asks.

"Big man said it was something about my appearance. Didn't like the look of me or something." Krehlborn, pulling his baggy leggings up.

"Same," Callum says, eating the wax treasure on his fingertip. "Said I was gunna gunk up the shiny toys. Prick."

Krehlborn shrugs his shoulders. "Beats scooping crap from the reindeer stables, you know? I'd take recovering lame Christmas presents from the postal service over that nasty business any day of the year."

The two elves laugh, working their way through the aisles.

Callum points to a big box wedged between several stacks of other packages. "Here. This one. Addressed to Lori from Ted. Jesus, it's big."

Krehlborn bends down and tries to tug the box free. "Heavy. Smells like complete ass, too."

"Let's make this a little easier," Callum says, snapping his fingers. The boxes float out of their way, and Krehlborn moves the big box to the center of the walkway.

The box is beat to bits, small impressions in the box bending it... *outwards?* Krehlborn thinks.

"Is it leaking?" he asks, investigating the sticky substance.

"It's leaking." Callum pokes the box with the tip of his scuffed black shoe, buckle jangling. The noise echoes throughout the warehouse.

The soft kicks from Callum's foot unleash a ghastly smell. The elves put their hands to their noses.

"Help…" a thin voice calls from the box.

The boys back up, their eyes wide.

"That box just talk?"

"It sure as shit did."

"Please…" the box continues. The voice is haggard, broken.

"Open it," Callum demands.

"You open it," Krehlborn replies, hands in the air. "You're the almighty leader for this one. You've got the tablet."

"The tablet doesn't—Christ, fine. I'll open it." He bends down, whipping a rusty box cutter from his pocket. "You just remember this next time we're at the bar and I ask 'Who's buying?'."

The knife slices through the tape, and Callum curls his fingers under the flaps of the top. He takes a breath and lifts.

"Good lord!" he shouts, jumping back.

"Lemme see," Krehlborn says, inching forward and peering over the open box, the smell radiating from it in waves.

"Jesus! Is it dead?" he asks, looking over at Callum in desperation.

The two peers in together, the cigarette finally taking the plunge from out of Krehlborn's mouth, tumbling into the open box.

Inside, a disheveled man wheezes, reeking of bodily fluids, looking like death warmed over.

"Help me… you gotta help me."

His eyes flutter beneath the bright red Santa cap, askew across his forehead. Below his chin, vomit has stuck in bits in his fake white beard, matting his paunchy red suit.

"Looks just like the big guy, eh?" Krehlborn says, nudging Callum in his ribs.

"Kinda does. Whaddya say we do with it?"

The two look at the man. Callum bends to check the delivery date.

"This guy shipped himself off five days ago."

"Definitely fell off the truck."

"The garbage truck, by the smell of it."

The man in the box begins to panic, finally realizing that he is staring into the faces of two magical beings. They are close enough to human, at any rate, but their black eyes and wide mouths filled with sharp teeth shine in the dim light of the warehouse.

"What the hell are you?" he shouts, gasping out his words in fetid puffs of air.

"Santa's helpers."

"Best and brightest."

The two laugh as if sharing the funniest joke. Their laughs, like nails scraping across the side of a car while the alarm goes off, send the man into a shiver.

Callum's eyebrows furrow as he reads his tablet.

"It says here you're due to be shipped to a Lori. You Ted?'

The man's eyes clear in realization.

"No, I'm—"

"Doesn't matter," Krehlborn says, cutting him off. "We'll get you where you're meant to go. But now that you've seen us…"

Callum picks up the hint. "I mean, he's already damaged goods."

The two cackle again, looming closer at the man in the soiled suit.

"Can't have him shaming our reputation to the big man or rest of the world or none of that."

Krehlborn whips his rusty box cutter up to his face. Callum nods in agreement. The man lets out a garbled scream.

The elf's hand jerks forward in a smooth slice. The man's neck opens up in a waterfall of crimson liquid, staining his white fake beard. The elves close the flaps, silencing the man's last gasps of air and sealing the box from end to end.

They heft the box back to their sleigh.

"Alright, buddy, time to pack it in. That's all there was here."

"Let's get these packages delivered."

The sleigh races through the night, sprinkling red droplets to the snow below from the leaking present.

Late or not, this package has a guaranteed delivery that the elves can't wait to enforce. Their fangs drip in delight, eyes crinkling in a hearty smile as they anticipate the joy they'll bring.

WIN BIG OR GET DEAD

Do you have what it takes to HalloWin? Theresa fought the urge to immediately tear the orange and black card in her hand to pieces.

"Halloween *and* a pun?" she mumbled. "Well, isn't this just the junkiest of mail." She sighed, rolling her shoulders which were sore from hoisting pumpkins around the farm all day.

Theresa turned the card over in her hand, impressed by the embossed text and thick cardstock. *Carve, bob, stuff your face, and run to $10,000!* the card proclaimed in an ornate font, blood dripping down the letters.

Holding the card up closer to her eyes, Theresa eyed the final line stamped on the card: a telephone number written in the smallest font.

The paper crumpled into a ball in her hands. Theresa was unwilling to give the sure-to-be scam another glance. She tossed the card into her wastebasket and set off to the kitchen to satiate her growling stomach.

As she walked through the kitchen to the backyard, Theresa caught a set of hushed tones in the living room. She paused, pretending to grab a glass of water, trying to overhear what her parents were saying.

Theresa winced her eyes shut, a lump forming in her throat as she realized they were discussing losing the farm—again. She'd moved back home after college to help her parents with the farm, but her degree in agriculture was as useful as the paper it was printed on when it came to her family's pumpkin patch. It had taken everything in her power to not just stay upstate, away from the farm and all its woes. She had even left her girlfriend, Rachel, behind. She remembered the tears in her eyes when she said she was heading back to her homestead to help her family out. How angry Rachel became that she had chosen the farm over a future in the city.

Theresa could hear her mother's stressed voice, crunching numbers out loud. She wanted to scream at them, tell them that they'd do much better with some other type of produce, but they wouldn't hear any of it. Not so long as they were Carvers. Their blood ran orange and their guts were stringy. There was no way around it.

Theresa's phone buzzed in her hand. She answered, hearing her best friend's voice from the other end.

"Did you get one?" April said, all but squealing into Theresa's ear.

"One what? A headache from your shrill voice?"

"No, shut up. An invitation!"

Theresa thought back to the balled-up card in the garbage can.

"Stupid little scam with lame little pumpkins boasting a fake contest?"

"You did! Jazzy said she got one too, and I just knew you had to have as well."

"Well, whatever it is, I don't want it."

Theresa could almost hear April rolling her eyes on the other end. "Why do you have to be such a Halloween humbug?" *Easy.* She'd watched it tear her family's savings into shreds every year, more and more, especially once the Jacks next door started using that god awful SuperGrow on their pumpkins. The Carver's organic and natural technique could hardly compete with three-foot-tall pumpkins colored an almost radioactive orange.

The Jacks had really outdone them all this year. A huge, five-foot pumpkin carved with the most wicked jack-o-lantern grin haunted her every day of the season. She knew that the Jack twins, Vince and Abe, had cut that smile into the giant pumpkin just for her.

She sighed, knowing April wasn't going to let this go anytime soon. She returned to her room, grabbing the paper from the trash and unfolding the edges.

"Did you call the number? The one that surely leads to an automated message on the other side ready to steal your social security number—and your mother's, while they're at it?"

Silence on the other end.

"April, did you?"

"…I did." She rushed her words, hoping to get them all out before Theresa started lecturing her on identity security. "But they were nice, and it sounds like a real legitimate situation. It's a contest that they're going to air as a Halloween special. They're setting it up in McKeene Woods, in that old, abandoned camping ground."

"Because that doesn't sound at all like certain death."

"C'mon, Theresa. Please? If it ends up being lame, we can hightail it home right away. And if it turns out to be true, we could win some big money."

Theresa contemplated her choices. Get stabbed in the face or have her friends angry at her for yet another Halloween?

"Fine. I'll call them and register."

April squealed. "Yes! Okay, Jazzy and I are going shopping for cute outfits later. Wanna come?"

"If I'm going to do this, I'll try and represent the farm in one of our very sexy polos. You two have fun."

Theresa felt her heart beat excitedly. Despite her reservations, she couldn't help but admit that April's enthusiasm was contagious and that this could be fun after all.

Theresa thought about calling Rachel, hoping that maybe she could talk her out of this weird commitment. But even as her excitement ran high, the pain of her heartbreak rang loud with warning.

Instead of calling Rachel, she dialed the number on the back of the card, heard some jaunty Halloween song about a spooky skeleton as a ringback tone. *Great start,* she thought.

After ten seconds of the cheery tune, an automated message started, the voice loud, deep, and sudden, causing Theresa to jump a little.

"Do you have what it takes to HalloWIN? If yes, press one. If you hate fun, hang up, and call back when you've grown a pair."

Theresa couldn't help but laugh at the audacity of the message.

She pressed one.

"Fan-spookin'-tastic!"

Theresa winced and pulled the phone a little further from her ear.

"On this Friday the 13th, make your way to McKeene camping grounds at 8:00 p.m. Be ready to sell your soul for a possible grand prize of $10,000! Five competitors will step in, but only one will HalloWin big!"

The phone clicked, the call ended, and Theresa felt a tickle of excitement (and maybe a little acid reflux) within her heart at the idea of contest.

Theresa's chest tightened as she approached the abandoned campgrounds, which looked far from desolate now. Spotlights and camera equipment littered the woods, pointed to different stations set-up with Halloween festivities.

April and Jazzy, wearing matching orange tank tops, were clasping their hands together, practically jumping up and down.

"Yay!" Jazzy said. "I can't wait to see who we are going to take down to win this money. We are going to absolutely slay this competition."

"Highly doubtful, farm freaks," Abe Jack said, walking out from the shadows with his twin brother, Vince, in tow.

Theresa placed her hand on her hip. "Really? 'Farm freak?' Aren't you two farmer boys?"

Vince scoffed. "Our agricultural business is art. Not that simple vegetable-growing you people do."

"No talent there. And I'm sure your negative profits reflect that," Abe said.

April groaned. "So glad the twins from Mt. Asshole have arrived."

Jazzy stepped forward. "We already planned on winning this thing. I'm just happy it's you we'll get to beat."

Theresa laughed at the standoff, which was looking more like the scene before an intense action sequence in a child's cartoon by the moment. "Alright, let's just get this thing over with. Has anyone seen a crew member yet?"

Within seconds of her finishing her statement and looking around, a voice boomed over a speaker from a tree overhead.

"Welcome to HalloWin! We've got a wonderful night ready for you. Please enter the first cabin where you will find the accessories needed for the show."

The five contestants walked up the cabin, Abe taking the lead and opening the door. The lights flickered overhead, illuminating a table with five round objects on it in front of them.

The lights turned on in a burst, momentarily blinding the group. A loud voice, distorted by an electronic voice box screeched behind them, causing the five to jump.

"Future victims! We're so happy you've arrived."

A thin figure, dressed from head to toe in black with a pumpkin mask bearing a cheerful grin, stood in the doorway.

"I'll be your host tonight, watching as you take on some Halloween activities and those Halloween activities take you out. One. By. One. Until… we're left with our winner, who will take home a hauntingly thick wad of cash! You can call me Gourdy."

Gourdy talked with the lilt of someone on a game show network, booming with confidence. Theresa felt unsettled at the voice, like listening to someone talk through the broken tubes of a static television.

"While you're here, you'll have to wear these beauties," Gourdy said, walking to a table adorned with five leather collars. "And before you ask, yes, they're shock collars. We've set up a perimeter around the campgrounds. If you pass it while wearing one of these, you'll get a nasty bit of electricity up and down your spine."

"What are we, sheep?" Abe asked.

"No, no. But we figured we'd raise the stakes for when things get a little dicey. Because they will." Gourdy leaned in close to them. "I'm just saying that for the ratings. Promise. You're probably going to see some stuff that looks real. But it's all just a gimmick. Swear on my seeds." The pumpkin mask stretched into a grin. "Some of you might even be in on it," Gourdy cackled.

Friend and enemy eyed each other a little more suspiciously than before.

"Where's the production crew?" Theresa asked, aware that it felt oddly empty in the campground despite a supposed live taping.

"We've got cameras strapped up all over the trees. All the better to catch you unaware."

Gourdy pointed at the collars. "Now, put those on and let's get tricky!"

The group snapped the large collars around their necks, feeling a bit like livestock. Theresa tugged at her collar, feeling the tightness close in around her throat a little too close for her comfort.

Gourdy exited the cabin. "Follow me for the first contest."

The contestants walked out back to the campground and towards five large barrels, bathed in a set of spotlights.

"Bobbing for apples, a classic favorite for all." Gourdy pointed to the barrels. "We're looking for three apples each. Last one to catch them all is eliminated."

The contestants took their places behind their barrels. Theresa tied her long hair back, stretching her neck muscles and working her jaw. April laughed at her antics.

"Ready and GO!"

Theresa shoved her face into the water, immediately trying to force one of the apples down to get a good bite into it, the edge of the barrel digging into her stomach. She heard splashing all around her as heads bobbed in and out of the wooden containers. She submerged her head again, pressing the apple to the side of the barrel and getting a grip at long last. She spat her first apple to the side, noting that Abe had already fetched two of his three. Everyone else was on their first.

Back into the water she went, grabbing her second point. *Just one more*, she thought, a grin escaping. She heard Abe cheering, clearly done with his task. Jazzy started hopping around, and April came in for a high five. She had to act fast—just she and Vince remained.

She dove in, wrangling another apple, pushing hard against the side, cursing her tiny mouth for making the task so difficult. With her head underwater, every sound was muffled. As her teeth bit down on the snappy skin of the fruit, Theresa heard the sound of happy hollers fade into screams. She emerged, apple in her mouth, and immediately whipped her head around.

The group was facing Vince, whose face was turning a terrible shade of green. He was clutching his neck, the muscles tensing visibly underneath his gnarled hands. Abe ran to his brother, concern squeezing his sharp features into even pointier shapes.

"Snake!" Jazzy yelled, as Theresa caught a glimpse of something black and thin slithering away into the woods.

"He's been bit," Abe growled. Vince sank to his knees, his hand coming away from his neck. Two tiny puncture wounds were evident on his skin, puckered and angry, thin lines of blood oozing from them.

Vince began to vomit, putrid water and bile spilling from his mouth, his eyes rolling into the back of his head.

"He needs help!" Abe shouted at Gourdy. "We need to get out of here now and get him to a hospital."

Gourdy clucked their tongue. "I'm afraid he's been eliminated, and the winners must move on." Gourdy put their hand to their cheek in a secretive motion, whispering to the contestants. "Remember, it's all showbiz."

"No way you're trying to pawn this off as fake. That water moccasin came out of that barrel and bit my brother. We have to go now."

"You could go with him. You could..." Gourdy waved a hand in Vince's direction, "...die with him."

Theresa's heart sank.

Gourdy continued. "Or you can keep playing the game. HalloWin, or get eliminated. It's simple."

Jazzy began sobbing as the rest of the group realized their predicament.

"You sick asshole," Abe shouted, tears running down his face. He started toward Gourdy. "I'm going to kill y—"

Gourdy dramatically removed a remote from their pocket, pressing down on a button. The collars on all the contestants released a shock, knocking them to their feet. Poor Vince, lying on the ground, convulsed, a froth coming from his mouth.

"Are we ready for Round Two?" Gourdy asked, pointing across the campsite to two picnic tables with four pumpkins set up on them. "My favorite." Gourdy's mouth opened into another wicked grin.

Theresa felt light-headed, trapped, unsure of what to do. She was positive this person was psychotic, and they were all at their sadistic whim. Maybe with some pumpkin carving, one of them could use whatever sharp instrument they were provided with to take Gourdy out.

She headed towards the tables, hoping the others would catch on. The group was silent, shocked with what they had witnessed, Abe shaking from head to toe in anger and grief. April put an arm around him, hoping to offer him some comfort.

Once at their stations, they sat down behind the pumpkin with their name on it. Theresa noticed the absence of a pumpkin for Vince, and the thought crossed her mind that this was all planned out. She cursed her stupidity for joining in on this game, when she had known it all sounded like a big scam. *This is far worse than getting a social security number stolen*, she thought morbidly.

"Okay, my little trick or treaters. For your next task, you must carve your pumpkin into a smile so big, it can be seen from the stars."

"Where are the carving tools?" April asked.

"True artists need no tools," Gourdy said. "Just the skill of a trained hand."

"Bullshit," Abe muttered, tears and snot staining his face.

"No foul language for the cameras, Abe. I'm only kidding. You'll find what you need inside the pumpkins. The last one to rip out all the guts and carve a wide smile into your little orange friends will be eliminated." Theresa noticed that the pumpkin stems already had a path cut out, an entry to the inside granted.

The four group members looked at each other, thoughts of self-preservation on their minds. Theresa could already see the animalistic fear written on their faces. Even her best friend. April, was looking at her like she didn't care if she lost, so long as she was one of the ones alive in the end.

"On your marks... get set... carve!" Gourdy yelled.

The four ripped the tops off their pumpkins and reached in.

"Ow!" Abe shrieked.

"What the—" April gasped out.

Jazzy let out a shrill scream.

With the lid off, Theresa reached into her pumpkin blindly and let out a pained yelp when she felt something sharp cut into her hand in several places. She removed her hand, holding it tight at the wrist. She saw three long gashes covering her hand.

"Jesus Christ, those are razor blades," April wheezed out through the pain, holding her own hand, dripping blood. Theresa peered inside, wishing she had looked within before sticking her hand down the neck of the gourd.

"You are dead," Abe said through gritted teeth.

"No time to be rude," Gourdy replied. "The clock is still ticking."

The group looked at one another, unwilling to put their hands back into the pumpkin.

"And what if we don't?" Jazzy asked.

Gourdy raised the remote up in their line of sight. "Zap, zap."

Theresa stood to try to get a better look inside before reaching in again and navigating her hand to one of the razor blades near the lip of the opening. She tugged, trying to free it. Her hand was shaking, and the blade was wet with pumpkin innards. She yanked as firmly as she could, and the thick rind of the pumpkin released the sharp metal.

Only three more blades to go. She went back in, cursing loudly as her hand slipped and another gash opened along the back of her hand. She heard other screams and yelps of pain, could hear Jazzy's sobs as the sharp edges cut her over and over as she tried to find the blades. Her panic blinded her.

Theresa freed the final blade, then began scooping guts from the pumpkin. She pulled them from the mouth, long and stringy, stained with her blood, making a pile on the table next to the removed blades. She saw Abe and April doing the same, having removed all the sharp parts inside their pumpkins.

Faster she scooped, thick strings wedging themselves under her nails, making them feel like they would pop off at any moment. Finally, there was nothing left to remove, so she picked up a discarded razor and began cutting a face into her pumpkin. She carved a line across the front of her the orange gourd, hoping it would be a wide enough grin to win.

Sweat rolled down her face, dripped off her nose as she maneuvered the blade over the pumpkin, her hand slipping and narrowly missing the path of the blade several times. Bloody fingerprints and smears adorned the face of the pumpkin, and her hand throbbed relentlessly as she carved.

She exhaled as the rind popped loose and she wedged the thick chunk free. With her pumpkin complete, she chanced a look at Abe, who had also completed the task. Saw April finishing the grin, a sigh of relief escaping her.

Relief that turned to dread as she saw Jazzy, eyes widening in realization and fear. Jazzy had never even finished removing the razor blades from the pumpkin, hadn't even started in on the guts.

Theresa watched in horror as Gourdy rushed over to Jazzy, their hand outstretched towards her head.

Jazzy tried to get up to run, Theresa following suit to try and charge Gourdy with a razor blade in each hand. Gourdy pressed the button on the remote, sending them all to back to their seats.

Theresa screamed as Gourdy placed a hand around the back of Jazzy's head and slammed her face into the pumpkin with enough force to blow it open. Jazzy's whine of pain was quickly muffled by the bits of pumpkin. Gourdy lifted her head from the carnage, her face slashed in several places from the razor blades.

April cried out for her friend as Gourdy slammed Jazzy's face into the pumpkin again and again, pulverizing the pumpkin and her head into a bloody, pulpy mess. Jazzy gurgled, choking on blood, fell limp to the table, dead.

Theresa felt tears running down her face and anger boiling her heart as Gourdy raised her friend once more from the table, shaking her corpse by the neck in glee.

"Now that's about as wide a grin as I could have hoped for," Gourdy said, a deranged lilt in their voice.

April sobbed and Abe turned his head from the carnage.

The rage dug into Theresa's stomach, rising to her throat. "You absolute lunatic!" she yelled in Gourdy's direction. "I'm going to kill you."

She ran as fast as she could towards Gourdy, who had dropped the remote in all their smashing fury.

"Kill you!" she shouted again, descending on the pumpkin person. Theresa lashed out with a razor blade, slicing deep into Gourdy's chest. A red streak appeared through the tight black clothes. Theresa breathed heavy, her hands dipping under the mask. "Gunna carve you up real good, you sicko." She attempted to lift the rubbery veneer, but her arms dropped suddenly to her side as her shock collar let out a strong electric current.

She heard April scream, shocked as well. But Abe... Abe was standing behind her, collar in one hand, remote in the other, an evil smile plastered across his face.

"Boo," he said, holding his mouth in an "o" for dramatic effect.

Theresa whipped her head back around as Gourdy started laughing from the ground, holding an arm across their chest.

"Told you there was an insider." With that, Vince, emerged from the trees. Gourdy chuckled. "Or two."

"You assholes," Theresa said through gritted teeth.

Vince pressed the button, shocking the girls once again. "Now that's not very nice."

At some point, April had made her way to her pulverized friend's side. "You killed Jazzy!" April sobbed.

"This is true," Gourdy said. "And we still have a game to play."

Theresa stood, confused and in pain. "What's going on? Why are you doing this?"

Abe shrugged. "Is not liking you or your piddly little farm not a good enough reason?"

Theresa was floored. "This is about the farm? The same farm that your family is driving out of business?"

"But also that first part," Vince said. "We just really don't like you."

"Gourdy here offered to set up a game for us. We thought it'd be fun. That'd you'd do anything for money." Abe walked close to Theresa, placing a hand under her chin. "We didn't know Gourdy was really going to knock you all off."

"But hey," Vince chimed in. "Better for business in the long run. Can you imagine the kind of foot traffic we can get to our business with a story like this? The merchandise?"

Theresa felt bile rise in her throat. "Why you?" she asked to Gourdy. "Who even are you?"

Theresa was met with a fierce silence, Gourdy's unwavering gaze, two triangular eyeholes dark with hatred burning her straight to her core.

Gourdy marched over to Theresa and April, grabbing the two by the arms. "Now, onto round three. Time to pit friend against friend."

All but dragging the two girls to the final picnic table, Gourdy planted them into a seat in front of two burlap sacks.

"Our final contest is one that will test your ability to engorge your own gourds. The first one to finish their candied meal wins the contest—and may escape with her life. But be warned; the two treats to choose from have their own caveats, so listen carefully. One bundle of fun is more alive than saccharine, and you'll be feeling them kick and scream all the way down."

Theresa shuddered. *Bugs*, she thought, watching the sack in front of her wiggling.

"Our second choice is a bag of delight, but if you don't properly check your candy, you just might burst at the seams." Gourdy stared deep into Theresa's face, who was scrunching her face in thought. "So what'll be: sweets for a sweet girl, or a good ol' fashioned bug-off?"

Theresa contemplated her choices. She knew April hated bugs, could barely stand to look at them. She felt responsible for the mess they were in.

"I'll take the bugs," Theresa said, watching April's face turn to one of relief. One last favor for a friend to give her a fighting chance.

"On the count of three, eat it all up!"

The girls positioned themselves at the mouth of the sacks.

"One," Gourdy said, crouching low and dramatically. "Two... and three!"

Theresa ripped open the mouth of the burlap and her stomach immediately rolled in protest. All she saw was legs—dozens of spindly, hairy legs. Legs bent and wiry.

Eat or die. Her decision made, she reached in, grabbing the first meaty spider she could and chomping down. The arachnid burst in her mouth, and she gagged at the acrid taste. She chewed, a leg protruding from her lips, which she sucked back in. She reached in again, a large grasshopper this time, feeling the crunch between her teeth. *God, how can I ever finish this all?*

The sack wriggled with what felt like a hundred insects stepping over each other. Theresa gazed at April, stuffing her face with chocolate and crystalized candies, one after another. *There's no way I can beat that.*

And she didn't. April finished her bag, hands in the air, tongue stuck out.

Gourdy clapped. "We have a winner!" Gourdy pulled the remote from their pocket. "Or do we?"

April's face fell. "I ate it all! I swear!"

"Oh, I'm most positive you did. Nothing left but wrappers. But did you check your candy? Tsk, tsk. I am a sucker for rules."

"No, no…" April started to cry, terrified at what her fate may be.

"One click of this remote, and we'll see if you obliged."

"Don't!" Theresa shouted.

April, turning grayer by the minute, locked eyes with Theresa. She looked uncomfortable, hands, held around her stomach.

"Kill this fu—" April started, but couldn't finish as her stomach exploded outward when Gourdy pressed the remote button with a single gloved finger. A charge of electricity ran through Theresa as she convulsed, watching a sizable hole blow through April's abdomen.

"If only she had skipped that piece of candy filled with sodium azide. Oh well, boom goes the loser."

Theresa pulled herself to her feet, charged at Gourdy with all her might, sending the remote flying through the air. Abe bent down to reach for it. Theresa grabbed his hand from her place on her stomach and bit down. She snagged the remote, whipped her arm back and threw it deep into the woods.

Vince went running after the remote, Abe looming towards her, Gourdy on the ground regaining the breath that had been knocked from their lungs.

Theresa ran. Her eyes wet with tears for her fallen friends, she sprinted through the woods in the direction of the farms. She'd hit one eventually, she was sure of it. She only hoped the perimeter wasn't truly rigged with an electrical fence at some point. The pain never came as she ran further from the campsite, and Theresa smirked at her called bluff.

In the distance she spotted the Jacks' barn. She nearly sobbed, entering, finding a pair of shears which she promptly used to cut off her collar.

She held the shears close to her chest, breathing heavily, hoping she had escaped.

Heavy footfalls outside the barn told her otherwise.

She positioned herself behind the barn door, kept quiet as Abe entered the barn. She jumped on his back, choked him with the collar, squeezing it tight around his neck. He wheezed and gasped under her hold

Vince ran into the barn, the remote held aloft in his hand.

He pressed the button, hoping to electrocute Theresa, but shocked Abe instead, who howled in pain. Vince received a shock of his own as he realized he'd harmed his twin, which Theresa took advantage of. She raised the shears, rescued from the floor of the barn, stabbed them into Vince's neck and pried them open, the force tearing through his skin.

She didn't wait to hear the sound of his head hitting the floor before returning to Abe, rising from the floor. She opened the shears wide and snipped, giving Abe a matching wound, cutting the head off the second snake.

Theresa ran from the barn, the shears in her hand. She saw the glowing light of the giant, five-foot jack-o-lantern ahead and sprinted towards it. Its grin taunted her from afar.

She climbed the back, her hands slippery with blood, making the task difficult. She finally reached the entrance and fell to a heap inside, just in time as Gourdy made their appearance on the path leading to the pumpkin.

Theresa's heart thumped wildly, sending silent prayers that Gourdy would walk past. Gourdy did—walked right past… then behind and up the throat of the giant pumpkin. Theresa turned, her back against the floor of the pumpkin, shears raised as Gourdy fell through the opening above.

Gourdy landed on Theresa, the shears piercing Gourdy's gut, continuing upwards from the force, eviscerating the figure to their throat. Blood rained down upon Theresa, who gagged as it entered her mouth and dripped into her eyes.

Gourdy was completely still. Dead. No chance for a last-minute villainous monologue.

Theresa pushed the body off her, noticing in that moment how familiar the limbs felt. She placed her fingers under the mask and lifted.

Theresa gasped loudly, her breaths turning into a heavy weeping as she saw Rachel's face underneath. In that moment, she mourned the death of her friends. All lost in the name of pumpkins, for the sake of a little Halloween fun.

As the last person standing, the only thing Theresa had won was a night of trauma and a lifetime of grief. In the heart of the pumpkin, Theresa's soul wilted, cut from the vine at last, covered in the blood of her ex-lover.

WOLFPIG, SHOW ME YOUR TEETH

As kids, it wasn't strange to own a stuffed animal or twelve, tattered by time and use and picnics with no real food to eat. Something to host a tea party for when family members are off doing what feels more responsible at the time.

Children hold these worn creatures tight in moments of fear, fling them about when overly excited, and discard them when it comes time to puff out their chests like big kids. Time to wipe those tears away, safe from public view.

My brother—I don't remember him well—was gifted my dearest possession in my youth: my soft, sweet Wolfpig who looked exactly how his name sounded. He should have kept my brother safe, but as it turns out, small toys meant for cuddles don't fare well against the power of flesh and blood.

Stuffed animals are the keepers of childhood, protecting people from the barrage of reality, waxing nostalgic about that security years later. Sometimes you wish you still had the furry creature to pull to your body, tight, warm, and musty. Sometimes that furry creature never left, occupying a place occasionally in your mind, but always in a box of history in your attic.

Sometimes, that furry creature stays with you, just off the corner of your vision, in your dreams, in your waking anxiety. Just there. Wolfpig was always just *there*.

In my dreams he was a strange wiggling thing, covered in fur with a curly Q tail. He was a slave to his captors, forced to dance and entertain. He'd fall from atop a table, straight onto his face, his hands shooting to cover his broken teeth as the crowd roared with laughter. The stubs and pieces of those teeth shot across the floor, blood splattering nearby. Wolfpig, my old friend, doomed by my psyche, bringing to his face the trauma of an innocent soul.

I'm thirty now, and I still remember that dream, my soft squirming friend humiliated and broken. My little Wolfpig dancing.

In my waking moments, I'd see him, bending towards me with a bloody mouth, pulled down in a silent scream. Though this tattered, stuffed, strange amalgamation of a creature was long gone, there he hovered, my fabrication threatening to wound me with his hooved and clawed hands, his pointed ears longing to hear my screams. As I stare into the viscera of his face, my ears hum and throb with a deep *kathoomkathoomthump*. He's pushing me somewhere, somewhere dark.

His presence has sent me to the edge. The edge of a life once lived. The edge of a memory, or at least more of a memory than I had before, of a time I'd swept under the bed. The edge between knowing that something bad had happened and remembering exactly what that something bad was and how that something bad felt and what that something bad meant.

It feels like I've been running my whole life on a treadmill, away from that edge. I spent twenty years running, just a dark void behind me. But now, he's looming, arms outstretched.

Since last week, Wolfpig has been more than there. He's amplified his hovering and breathing and waiting and he's begun *chasing*. All I can do is open my mouth and scream silently.

Today, I came home from work, my car covered in the garage. I emerged from the metal frame, gently closing the door behind me, and immediately felt him in the room. I turned my head, his shadow standing in the corner, shielded by rakes and brooms. He burst through, and he chased me, calling for my skin, my flesh, my teeth. My memory. I felt his hot, labored breath in my ears, on my neck, as if he was everywhere at the same time. His teeth on my shoulder; I slap away a snout, but there's nothing there to connect with.

He chases me and I run to my room, slide under my bed, arms at awkward angles at my sides. So much harder to fit under here than when I was a child. I shiver in the darkness, seeing the clawed hooves of his hind legs just in view from under the bed. A weight above as he jumps on top of the mattress. He circles, curls up like a dog on a blanket, bending the bed towards me underneath. I hear his snorts. My body is frozen as I recall the last time I was under this bed.

I sit in my shame. The world collapses around me, goes dark like curtains closing on a stage, forcing me inwards.

My brother—I still don't remember him well, but I remember this moment—screamed when he was four. He was taken by our father, crazed and in anger. My brother looked too much like my mother, not enough like my father, so my father let the drugs do the talking. My brother stood no chance. He was taken; he was murdered. This… this is what I knew.

But as Wolfpig roars and croaks above me, chasing me deeper into my mind even as I sit huddled on the floor, I'm pushed further.

I'm shown how I sat, crouched, under my bed, unable to move, to do anything a big sister could. *Should.* How I watched as my father scooped my brother's tiny body into his arms. Took him from the room.

How there were no words uttered, but soft gasps of air fell from lips too small to speak up and stop what was happening. Louder exhalations from a body spurred by toxins, doing the unthinkable and harming his own flesh and blood.

I'm pushed further into the deep, seeing how I remained, until morning, under that bed. Didn't call for help. Didn't tell Mom when she got home from work. Didn't give details once my brother was proclaimed to be missing. Didn't. Didn't. Didn't.

What I knew meets what I now know.

All they found were his teeth, broken, cracked, displaced. Childhood was snuffed from him, whisked away by pointless rage. The small, stuffed animal I'd tucked under his arm at night didn't stop it from happening.

I was too young to grieve then. But now, I do. For my little Wolfpig.

My father, he was caught eventually. Overcome with what he'd done. He's paid his price.

My memories have caught me. Overcome with what I didn't do. I'm paying mine.

The increasingly frenetic appearances of Wolfpig as I drift to sleep at night and wake in the morning force memories forward. Wolfpig, with his mouth dripping blood, whispers to me, overcoming the repeated thrum of pressure in my ears. I vaguely hear him commanding me to move. Telling me to run. Urging me to help.

He leans in and I feel his fetid breath wetting my face with his dripping, broken teeth. *Move. Run. Help.*

So, I do. I move into the darkness. I run into my past. I help my brother.

I force myself into my mind where I know Wolfpig exists. And maybe he's there and we, together, can protect my brother from his fate.

I'm neither here nor there, awake or asleep, just a visitor trapped in my own headspace. A vacationer already feeling like I've overstayed my welcome.

I see him ahead, his furry body larger than I remember. His snout, long and thin like a dog's but flat like a pig's, is pointed in the air, sniffing, sensing my presence. He's no longer chasing me. He's waiting, in front of me now, and I'm lunging for him.

I watch his tail, wagging ahead, its curl indicating where I should be going. I pick up my pace, stop when I feel a hard pebble under my bare foot. I catch a glimpse of another falling from Wolfpig's body, leaving a trail. White pebbles fall, and I chase them like a kid following a forest floor filled with candy before entering a house full of witches. I walk up to one, pick it up, turn it over in my hands. I feel the rough cuts and divots, the smooth surface in front, the long root below.

Not pebbles. Not candy. Wolfpig is leaving a trail of teeth.

Put them back where they belong, I feel him say to me, his voice creaking over the crevices of my brain, turning over the thoughts and searching for a place to grab hold. I don't know if he's referring to the memories or the teeth themselves.

I do both.

I crawl, pick up another discarded tooth. Another. And soon my hand is full, the weight of their existence like a handful of pill bugs, squirming. They click as they hit each other, moved by my hand, trembling as I bring it to my mouth.

The teeth enter, my cheeks packed like a rodent's full of physical objects that were never mine but are now a part of me. They float in my saliva. I breathe through my nose.

I follow Wolfpig deeper, placing the tiny teeth he leaves behind into my mouth one at a time, space in my mouth becoming a more finite resource. The memories hit me harder, no longer just repeated images of my brother hitting the ground, but the emotions I've long forgotten tied to the pictures, like bringing music to silent films.

Finally, Wolfpig stops. In front of him, a bed. He crawls under, lifts the sheet to invite me in. I get on my knees and enter, my mouth still full of teeth. Some swallowed completely, swimming in my gut. Others are lodged in my throat.

We lay together, under the bed. He reaches his hands out, gnarled claws grazing my forearm. His snout presses into my forehead.

I take what he offers. More teeth, small, like a child's. Broken.

I swallow what's left in my mouth, the hard edges cutting my throat on the way down. I replace the emptiness with Wolfpig's gift, the small teeth finding purchase in my gums.

They grow, filling my mouth. Top descends into bottom, bottom finds roots and pins to the top. My mouth is sealed shut.

I forget to breathe. Couldn't if I tried as Wolfpig holds a paw-hoof to my nose. With his other hand, he holds my own, my hand clasping around the smooth, cylindrical shape, feeling his paper-thin fur stuck to the outside.

I suffocate slowly, the bed disappearing from overhead, exposing me for what I am.

I know that I'll be found eventually, shame and all, memories and all, guilt and all. I'll be heavier than I was before.

Wolfpig moves his claw from my nose to my mouth, pries open my lips, digs the point of his hoof into my mouth. He reaches inside, my tongue lolling underneath. His body tastes like a mushroom, filled with soil. His fur tickles my cheeks, like a wire brush gone limp.

Deeper he goes, smoothing his hoof against my tongue. I feel the tip of him reach the back of my throat. He curls his hand, presses on the distinct part of my tongue that makes me gag in response.

I vomit.

Teeth surge forward, spat onto Wolfpig's body, the floor, my own chest. Hundreds of teeth, some bone-white, some rot yellow. A few pieces linger and they roll in my mouth. I spit them out into the puddle.

I've consumed, been consumed, unconsumed. Regurgitated memories free of their acid cage.

I grip the hoof that remains in my hand, watching as Wolfpig begins to fade. The bed that we crept under together is a different bed now. My own.

I stare into Wolfpig's eyes, deep and crusted. We know each other now.

Just like before, like always, stuffed animals are the keepers of childhood, protecting people from the barrage of reality. Sometimes you wish you still had the furry creature to pull to your body, tight, warm, and musty. Sometimes you do have it, close enough to pull to your skin.

Finally, Wolfpig disappears, his hoof replaced by an orange tube, lid off.

I'm on my wooden floor, surrounded by the stink of vomit, by small objects that were once inside me, now out, exposed like my memories for the toxin they are.

The once-full pill bottle crumbles to the floor, the two remaining pills clacking against the plastic sides like small, broken teeth.

THE PITS

"Again?" Leslie asks, placing a hand on my shoulder. "You just checked last night."

I freeze, my fingers still cupping my breast, pressed gently into the skin. She's right. But after my mother's diagnosis, I just can't shake the feeling that my own is waiting for me on the front doorstep, a box gift-wrapped and addressed to me straight from the genetics department or God or whatever force out there decides our fate.

"I know, but I thought… I thought I felt something." I shift my hand, working my fingers into the side of my breast, up into my armpit, damp from perspiration as my anxiety ramps up. I push, timidly, palpating the flesh to the tissue underneath.

"You're going to *make* something appear, Kels, you keep aggravating your body like that."

My partner isn't entirely wrong. I've been known to irritate a lymph node in the past, worrying that I felt the lump growing under my touch, pushing it beneath my skin, back and forth across muscle and tendon. Each time, my fears were only slightly assuaged by an ultrasound or doctor's opinion. Only slightly, because, well, The Internet.

As soon as I became aware of just how fragile bodies are and aged into being my own health advocate, I found it difficult to convince myself that certain death wasn't around the corner with every stray lump, every cough that lingered too long, every *thing* that felt in the least bit *off*. We train ourselves to listen to our cars for each strange sound or to feel for unwarranted shaking on the road and to keep up on regular maintenance. I've trained myself to do the same with my body.

"There. I know I feel something. Leslie, here. Put your fingers here."

"In your armpit? Kels, I love you and I know we're going to be married soon, but there are still some places I just don't want to go. Especially not at eight in the morning."

"For the love of—" I grab Leslie's arm. "Here. Just wash your hand after. The pit won't bite."

Leslie groans, and then accommodates my demand.

Her fingers press gently into the underside of my arm. "Huh. I guess I do feel a little something."

My eyebrows shoot to my forehead.

"I wouldn't worry though. It's probably just an irritated lymph node." She can sense my worry. "I'd be irritated too if I had to be stuck in you. Especially right there." She points to my pit. "In that," she jabbed a finger at me, "stinky, stinky pit." She winks.

I hold my hand to my chest, feigning hurt. "Hey! You're such a rude-ass."

"You love me."

I give her a chaste kiss. "I do." I put my shirt on and proceed to get ready for work. *Just keep an eye on it,* I think, trying to keep myself from getting worked up. *It's probably nothing.*

Throughout the day, I try to keep the thought of the lump out of my head. At some point, the refrain of *it's probably nothing* shifts to *it's definitely something* so I call my primary care and make an appointment to get it looked at. At least to rule out the possibility of it being something worse. It won't be the first time I've made an appointment for something to have a doctor look at it and dismiss it. It's almost always been a lump of some kind, and it's almost always gone away at some point with no treatment, only to reappear somewhere else. Medicine considers it having gone away as a non-problem, but to me, the reappearance is cause for concern. But I have to trust myself, especially with my mom's recent diagnosis. *Maybe now they'll take it seriously.*

With my errands complete, I arrive at the lecture hall just in time to load my slides and take a couple of deep breaths before starting the discussion for the day. I stare out into the sea of young faces in front of me, trying not to think about what they're thinking about me as I try to liven up the discussion on cartography's modern history.

Whenever I stand in front of the classroom, I'm always amazed that this was my chosen career. That I, Kelsey of Anxietyville, opted to become a college professor and speak in front of large crowds for a living. The talking, that was never a problem. I love maps and geography and I've always been excited to impart my wisdom on the next generation of cartographers. But the thinking…

I start the lecture in earnest. *Do the students think I'm too old to be dressing the way that I do? (At least I'm comfortable.) Do they expect a woman to wear heels and a dress?* Even though my mouth is moving and I am fielding questions from the students with ease, my mind fills with bursts of thoughts. *Can they tell I'm gay? (You are, though). Does it matter if they can tell I'm gay?(It shouldn't, but it does.) Who's going to address me as "Mrs." today? (I have a doctorate, dammit.)*

The thoughts are constant, some fleeting. Others come back for me to think about during a long shower or at night when sleep escapes me. They spin around, until I feel like I, too, am physically spinning, caught in a whirlwind but feeling frozen in place.

The anxiety bubbles up inside of me, causing a fine layer of sweat to form across my body, which then produces more anxiety as I wonder if the students can see it and what they say about me behind my back.

It's never-ending.

"So, as you all can see, computer software has made the art of mapping a little bit easier nowadays. But that doesn't mean—" I stop suddenly, feeling something squirm in my armpit.

"Mrs. Adams, are you okay?"

The feeling of something unnatural taking residence in the upper crook of my arm grabs ahold of me. I don't even have the energy to correct the student. I raise my hand to the offending area, waiting for it to move again. It doesn't.

"I'm fine," I say. "Sorry, just a little cramp or something. Guess I'm getting too long-winded about maps. Happens all the time." I earn a chuckle from some of the students. I force a smile, trying to forget the sensation of something wiggling under my skin. I can't wait to get back to my office so I can close the door and see if it is just a product of my imagination or something real.

"All right, well, we're just about at the end of the discussion today. How about we pack it up a few minutes early? See you all Thursday." As soon as I start speaking, the class begins shoving books and computers into bags. The shuffling is always immediate and overwhelming, and I dread the days I have to shout over it to make announcements.

With the class empty, I make my way towards the door, bundling my books in my arms, my shoulder bag bouncing off my hip. I walk briskly, head tucked, avoiding long-winded conversations with colleagues along the way. I burst into my building, up the stairs to my office, shut the door, and strip my shirt from my body. I raise my left arm and crane my neck in an angle that still forces me to jut my eyes all the way to the side of their sockets so I can get a good look. I run my hands up and down the exposed area, searching for the invader. I can still feel the lingering crawling sensation of what felt like a grub on my skin, but I see nothing that suggests it was ever there.

My heart rate begins to slow once I decide that it must have just been a weird nerve thing. Never mind that it was in the same armpit as the small lump I'd discovered this morning. I need to quiet the thoughts, the voices that scream *death* between my ears. Deep breaths. I think of Leslie, her gentle brown eyes, her voice soothing the thoughts in my head. Picturing us breathing together; the anxiety quiets.

I sit at my desk and attempt to get some work done. Grading papers, sending emails, even completing a small amount of writing for my next journal article, I barely notice as the time flies by and it's soon the dinner hour. I pack my things and head to my car.

Two days later, I sit in the sterile, white-walled office of my doctor, my torso disrobed, covered in a thin paper gown. I press my fingers into my armpit, feeling for the offending lump. It's there, slightly swollen, but no larger than before.

The doctor walks in.

"How are we doing today, Kelsey?" he asks, a smile on his face.

"Doing okay. Work, getting ready for the wedding. Always something burning on the stove, you know?

He chuckles. "I do. I wish you and Leslie the best on the big day." He shifts on his rickety metal stool. "So what brings you here today?"

I frown, the worry kicking in. "Well, my mom was recently diagnosed with breast cancer, so I've been extra vigilant in checking for early signs. I noticed a lump under my armpit."

"Hmm," he says, reaching forward. "May I?" I nod, and he massages the area. "It feels soft, and I can feel the definition of a lump there. But see how the skin is irritated?"

"Probably my fault for prodding," I say, sheepishly.

"No, it looks irritated deeper than that, more like an infection."

"So... not cancer?" I ask, hopefully.

"More indicative of something else. But we can run some labs and order an ultrasound."

He must have caught the look of fear on my face.

"Just to rule out the worst," he continues. He flips through my chart. "This isn't the first time you've come in for something like this, right?"

"Well, no." I feel caught. Like I've made a mistake coming here. "But this one feels different, like something growing, moving."

As soon as I say it, I feel the anxiety start to kick up.

"Well, considering your family history—which I'm very sorry for, by the way—it's good to get it checked out. But this just feels like a lymph node doing its job. Absorbing some kind of infection. It's movable, soft, with a bean shape, so other than its size, nothing is out of the norm."

The more he talks, the sillier I feel, and the nerves start gnawing at my gut that I'm—God, I don't even want to think it—*hysterical* for coming in. Did I really feel it move? As my stress continues in earnest, I almost swear I can feel the lump vibrating again, swelling within. I want to grab the doctor's hand and make him feel what I feel. Maybe I can—

"Okay, Ms. Adams. I'll order some labs and an ultrasound for you and then we can discuss them at your next appointment which you can schedule out front." Before I can say anything else, he's out the door. Guess my fifteen minutes of appointment are up.

I try to calm my nerves, breathing before I dress and make my way to the front desk. The oscillations in my armpit have stopped once again, but the thought of being overly neurotic lingers.

In a few minutes, I'm on my way home when my phone lights up and I answer Leslie's incoming call.

"How much do you love me?" she asks as the line connects.

"A lot. But even more if you tell me you picked up some burritos for the night."

"Good, ultimate loving then. I also picked up that new scary movie so we can not only eat burritos, but also be burritos in bed."

I smile. "I'll be your tortilla if you get too scared."

"That's what I thought."

"I'll be home in a few."

"Love you."

She hangs up and I keep my eyes on the road, sighing in contentment.

My phone chirps and an email pops up on the screen. It's from my department chair. The subject line reads: *Tenure File*. My heart jumps into my throat and then plummets to my stomach. The shallow breaths begin as I wait until I hit a stoplight, and then open the email.

"Son of a bitch!" I scream after reading the email. I *knew* they'd pull this crap. Despite having strong student evaluations and a consistent publishing record, they—they being the tenure committee, comprised solely of bitter, old men—have given me a poor rating. It's all just an artificial attempt to keep their budget down and save promotion and security for—

BEEEEP!

The car behind me honks, long and loud, and I realize that the light has turned green. In my anger, I hold my hand up in apology and drive.

It doesn't take long for the anger to turn into stress. Stress about my job, about being an impostor, wondering if I'll ever break through the boy's club of our department. The worry gnaws at me, roiling my stomach.

Something wiggles within.

More full-bodied than before, my arm feels heavy, feels like something is not only moving, but growing within the fragile stubble-filled flesh of my armpit. Keeping one shaking hand on the steering wheel, I move my arm and explore, and this time, I touch something that shouldn't be there.

I feel it, through my clothes, squirming. The size of a lima bean, the intrusion is soft and warm. I try to shift my gaze to the side, but I can't see it. Can't get an eye on what feels like a chunky worm beneath my skin. Can't…

I force my eyes onto the road, a good thing as my bumper creeps a little too close to the car in front me. The offending pressure in my armpit lessens as I coerce my mind to focus on getting home safely.

Just a few more miles. The twisting, throbbing sensation stops.

I pull my car into the driveway and fly from my vehicle, bursting in the front door.

"Leslie?" I call out. Her car's in the driveway, but I don't see her anywhere in the house. "Leslie?!" I call out louder. My pulse hastens and the squirming in my armpit starts again.

"Kels? I'm right here." Leslie appears in the kitchen, closing the sliding glass door behind her. She notes my pallid skin. "You okay?"

"I felt… there was something…" I don't know how to explain it, worrying that despite how much she loves me, she'll just chide me for being a worrywart again. I stuff it down.

"I just had a long day," I finally say.

Leslie doesn't press me for more. Instead, she gives me a hug, and God bless her doesn't balk at the dampness of my clothes.

"Burritos in burrito bedsheets?" she asks.

I nod in response, and we head upstairs for a scary movie in bed.

I make it through the night, enjoying the snuggles and calm. I tell Leslie about the appointment. After a long rant about my job, I force the tenure email from my head. I chalk up the weird arm issue to anxiety about the lump and being overworked. Explain it away. Don't give in to the incessant nagging that something is wrong.

Leslie is asleep next to me. I try to close my eyes, but my mind is racing. I feel myself trapped between a state of half-sleep and wide-awake. My mind eases just enough, letting its guard down, and everything floods in. Grading that's past due. Job security. The impending wedding. Weight gain. Aging. My mom's diagnosis.

It all. Comes. Crashing down.

My breathing speeds up, and soon, I've soaked the sheets through with my sweat. Leslie snores softly beside me and I find myself paralyzed, unable to move.

The movement in my left arm starts again, suddenly, and with more force than before. Trapped in my frozen state, my arms remain at my sides. The squirming turns into writhing, and the writhing builds momentum, the source expanding by the second. It moves beneath my skin. No way that's some swollen lymph node. Something is *alive*.

I start to whine, a low sound that sharply ends in a squawk. I finally will my arm to move and I stroke the skin of my armpit, crying out when I feel how large the twisting lump has grown. Leslie still snores beside me, smacking her lips.

I force my arm to rise and look leftward, thankful for the tank top I'm wearing. I finally see it. A bubbling, twitching mass. What was once a single lump seems to have sprouted more, pulsating under the thin and sensitive skin of my armpit. The space feels full, a betrayal of the normally hollow concavity of the area.

My heart beats faster than ever, barely able to keep up with the storm of anxiety wracking my body. The more anxious I get, the bigger it grows. The mass expands and squirms, gestating in my stress, feeding off the energy and loathing and confusion and panic. I watch it grow by the second, feeling it swell with every wave of stress and hotness that flushes across my body.

I cry out again, tears blotting my cheeks as I struggle to comprehend what I'm seeing and feeling, the wriggling descending into a storm of pain centered on its form. With my alarmed shout, Leslie stirs at long last, turns over blearily, and takes me in, her eyes opening widely when she sees me.

"I can't—it won't stop!" I shout.

"What the hell is that?" Leslie asks, horrified.

"It just appeared! I don't know! But God, it hurts!"

As Leslie looks down at me, fear in her eyes, I feel the anxiety accelerate. It terrifies me to have her look at me with unabashed fear on her face.

The thing inside me grows again.

It's the size of a lime, still moving in circles, wrapping around on itself.

Leslie screams as it presses its face against my skin, pushing it outwards.

I scream as it burrows and twists.

I'm a monster. I'm going to die. Leslie's going to catch it. Leslie will die.

The thoughts twirl around my brain, barraging me with their burden. I stare into Leslie's eyes. *What if I lose her?*

The thought of it all, the uncertainty of what is happening, sends me into a shock, at the height of my frenzied state. It bursts through the skin of my armpit.

It lands with a soft *plump* on the top sheet of the bed, letting out a shrill cry. Blood pours from the gaping wound, the hole left by the creature large enough that it feels like it's almost severed my arm. Leslie stares at me and quickly wads up the sheet and forces it against my skin to stem the bleeding, the cotton filling the void the creature created. I stare at the thing.

Sliding around on the bedsheet, the gray form is slimy and covered in a thin layer of viscera. It gurgles from inside its core. Still wiggling, pulsating, matured to the size of a baseball, the mass looks back at me, though it has no eyes. I see it for what it is.

The ugly thing I carry inside, given physical form. Fears, unseated.

We scream at each other, our faces inches apart.

Leslie smashes it with a book. The gray thing explodes. The cancerous pieces, the rotting thoughts fly through the air, sticking to walls, to us.

I'm still screaming, blood pooling into the sheet tucked under my arm. Leslie is holding me as I sob, releasing what I've bottled inside.

The same story, echoing.

It starts as a lump. It becomes a monster, holding tight. Always in the back of your mind until it forces itself to forefront. It coils. It doubts.

It dies.

PINS AND NEEDLES

Tiny bright fireflies dance around my vision. They're stars, then fireflies, then stars again. White specks across a pitch-black night.

That interstitial blinking, the fuzziness of it all, mimics the way the rest of my body feels. Heaviness like a weighted blanket, one built of metal and mud, falls over me. All limbs nonresponsive, it's enough work just to make my body breathe. Not sure which animals can hear me choking on air out here, wherever I am beneath the night sky. Can barely blink, tears cornering the hollow spaces of my eyes, then dropping down the sides of my face and into ears that can't hear yet.

But I can think, and I can remember.

Remember how I died.

Remember how I died again.

Every time, my body relearns how to work in the process of me recalling how I died, moment by painful moment. I don't know if what I am is immortal, or lucky, or just really, really *unlucky*, but I'm running out of ways to see how permanent death is for me. For some ungodly reason, death is as fleeting as a thought, jumping from between your fingers in the early morning rise.

I've woken up like this, a dozen times before, on my back, spit up from whatever literally death-defying stunt I've taken on. Or maybe 'death-defying' isn't the proper term. I think what I go through is death—it just doesn't quite stick.

I'll spend what feels like an eternity watching monsters dance around me, my mind likely grappling with an unconscious that's trying to fade, creating a horrific display of background noise. What was last in my thoughts is blown to terrifying proportions as whatever life is tries to tick away. It drops like the last grain in an hourglass to a pile of used dirt below, but then I'm clawing my way back through the pinprick. Alive. Re-Alive.

I lie on the ground, my eyes watching the fireflies and stars, and I think about how those stars are me. Visually dead. Noticeably withering. Just traveling the distance into some sort of existence before our eyes. I wait to see what comes back and what memories they bring as they do. It begins.

My hands come alive first. As I tense my wrist and grip imaginary objects with my fingers, the prickling begins. My hands remember the way it felt to ward off pockets of air, swimming in nothing but the wind circling me.

Toes wiggle about, powered by the tendons in my feet, reminding me of how they felt, running, then jumping from the edge of the cliff to the water below. They left footprints behind me as they *plap plap plap*ped to the side, pushing off with one last hurrah. I suspect this death will live in my memory, the uniqueness of solid ground underfoot juxtaposed by the long plummet of freefall etched into my bones.

My arms, pins and needles as I lie here on the dirt. Dirt beneath my shoulder blades, I can feel that now as my back wakes up, sharp shocks down my spine. It feels now how it did last night when my back slapped against the water after falling a hundred feet, no more forgiving than a cement floor after a nudge out the window to the street below. The sensation, though short-lived, felt like it catapulted my bones from back to front, and I half-expected to see them flying through the air.

Legs transform from leaden weights, no longer stiff tree trunks laying parallel with the shore below me, but instead jolting awake, like matches struck against a rough surface and dancing with fire. They remember the feeling of inactivity, uselessness from a spine shattered by my descent to the water below. Sinking, but unable to kick. Unable to push me back to the surface with what little awareness I had left.

Breathing becomes easier, no longer counting as I breathe, timing breaths to slow a heart beating all too rapidly for being completely still minutes ago. My lungs constrict, remembering the feeling of air flushed from their cavity, making room for murky water.

My stomach wakes up next. It roils with lake water, swallowed hours ago. I became a part of that lake, and that lake lived inside me, but apparently, we aren't compatible after all. I vomit, water surging from my gut and out my mouth, and the volume is so extreme I wonder if I'll spit out a fish or turtle or a couple of rocks. I don't, but my throat burns, now fully alive, from the strain.

I shift, rocks making their presence known beneath my back and arms. The pins and needles drift away, my body no longer numb, but alert with the resurgence of my mind.

Falling beats death. Drowning beats death. Two birds with one stone, killed deader than I'm beginning to realize I'll ever be.

I wonder why I test its limits. Why I do it over and over again. What happens if it stays? If I test it and it gives me a different answer than it has before, and I don't come back again?

My hands dig into the soft dirt around me, savoring the feeling of grit between my fingers. Questions for another day, I suppose.

Today, I rise.

DOUBLING DOWN

"Did hamburger buns really do him in?" Paul brought the drink to his lips, contemplating the stupidity of the now-incarcerated third member of their weekly barstool confessional group. Rosie nodded, sitting next to him. "Leaving a footprint in a bag of spilled buns," he continued, shaking his head.

"Allegedly," Rosie's voice bubbled from behind her cocktail.

"Allegedly. Can't believe what those shows say anymore. I hear you. Christ. Okay, well, I guess anything's a death sentence these days."

The pair sipped their drinks in silence, letting the minutes pass over them. They valued the moments of freedom they had, knowing how fragile time could be. They saw to it that others knew, too. Time betrays their victims, unconcerned with her fickleness. *I'll install that camera next week*, they think. *No need to fix that lock today.* Their own demise.

Paul quietly sipped his beer. The headlines were starting to pick up on his activity. *The Spine Stalker*, the headlines boasted, referencing his method of killing. A missing vertebra at every scene, working his way from bottom to top.

Rosie had managed to keep her murders off the radar so far. Turns out when you're a revenge killer, the people who get dead have a lot of reasons for it.

Paul admired Rosie. Her kills were always clean. He fed off her ability to do what she did in such silence. No fanfare. Just art.

"Your last guy really deserved it, eh?" Paul asked, swiveling on his barstool.

Rosie smiled, her mouth a crooked smirk. "You wanna hear the story again? I know I told it just last week, but man, the look on your face."

Paul felt his heart speed up, hoping he could get that feeling again. Her story, his story; her revenge, his success. Her glory, his.

She put her lips around the tip of her straw, her thick drink slowly working its way up the plastic and into her mouth. She swallowed, embellishing the refreshing satisfaction of her ice-cold alcohol. "I stabbed him in the gut in his garage. Caught him as he was cutting the brakes on his wife's car."

Paul groaned. "Tell it better."

Placing her drink back onto the counter, she put her hands up in the air in a "surrender" motion. "So damn demanding, Paul. Fine, fine. From the start." Rosie leaned forward, elbows on the counter, eyes sparkling. "I was belly-down in his garage. Thinking about how telegraphed the last weeks of his life were. How I'd watched him plan this murder attempt from afar. Watched him as he searched automotive parts on the Internet, scratching his scraggly beard. Watched as he stared down his wife, and she mistook it for fiery passion.

"I'm real quiet, as you're aware, so I knew, with my stomach cold against the smooth cement, that he was a doomed man by my hands. He was dead as soon as I figured out which day he was going to do it, which day he had an extra pep in his step."

Paul held onto her every word.

"The stalk," she started, "is half the fun," the two said in unison, both letting out a chuckle afterwards.

Rosie continued her story. "Before he gets home, I sneak into his garage—one of those manual doors makes it real easy. I creep under his wife's car, parked in place. She was preparing a nice meal for him, so she wasn't leaving anytime soon.

"I hear them argue. They always do. Loudly. He tells her he's going to go tinker around in the garage, work at his bench on something productive—'Unlike our marriage!' he yells at her. My midsection is in knots, ready to get him real good.

"He walks to the garage, slams the door all dramatic-like. Goes right for her car, forces open the hood. I hear him make a few snips, know he's doing the deed to get his wife hurt or killed. He bends under the car, and our eyes meet. I've got my knife in all its double-bladed glory by my side, and before he knows it, before he even has time to holler, I've struck out at his eyes. Got one slashed flush across its width. Pops like a gooey tire.

"His hands go to his face. My blade goes to his heel. I slice a tendon, clean, and he goes down like he's been hit by a linebacker. I make sure he knows with every stab that this is revenge for what he's done to her over a lifetime of misery. Pre-revenge for what he was going to do."

Paul flashed white teeth Rosie's way. "Gets better every time I hear it. Chills, right up my spine. Right where I like 'em."

The two sat, ruminating in the wake of Rosie's tale of destruction.

"You pick a place?" Rosie broke the silence, her drink nothing more than a dribble of slush at the bottom of the glass.

"Little spot off the road. Few trees, no close neighbors."

"She single?"

"As always."

Rosie nodded, approving of Paul's details. "Good choices. A lot like my next victim. Must be something in the air."

"Must be the same thing that's always in the air." Paul winked behind his beer, sucking in the last sip.

"Good luck on your job," Rosie said, placing a few dollars on the bar top.

Paul stood up, putting his ballcap on his head, shrugging his shoulders through his jacket. "See you next week."

Paul walked through the empty canal toward his destination. He traveled light with only his switchblade in his pocket, gloves on his hands, worn ballcap snug atop his head. The walk was long, winding, carefully planned to take him the backway to his target's home. The air was chilly.

He walked, wondering if this one would scream. He knew she was sleeping soon—she'd declared herself a certified grandma at the AA meeting they'd both attended earlier that week. He found the best subjects there, struggling, unfocused, vulnerable. His feigned story of sobriety took him from meeting to meeting sifting through the groups, letting their sob stories lead him on his journey.

She was perfect. His type. And he was almost at her house.

Pondering who Rosie would be hitting tonight, Paul walked up to the backdoor of his victim's house. Sneak in, quietly, slide the screen ever so slightly. The smooth sound as the door ran across the track reminded Paul of the introduction of a serrated knife through clothes, and goosebumps dotted his skin. In he went. Out of the dark and into the shadows.

He walked through the house, silent so as not to alarm the sleeping woman. One could never factor in a light sleeper or a restless night spent staring at the ceiling. He crept about, noting the pictureless walls, the blandness of it all. It could be as much his home as it was hers. He ran his fingertips across the bare plaster, his gloves leaving nothing behind.

His hand appeared in the doorway, and then Paul curved his neck to peer around the frame. She was there, sleeping, a book balanced on her last read page spread open next to her prone form. As he reached towards her face, her eyes shot open.

She let out a short-stopped scream, muffled by his gloved hand, the useless noises dying as they were absorbed into his palm. Wordlessly, he replaced his hand with a piece of duct tape, placed snugly over her lips. He could see her tongue working behind the tape as she attempted to wet it, pry it off. He glanced at the book, undisturbed next to her, noting the true crime genre. *Let's hope she isn't a quick study*, he thought.

His knees on either side of her body, now flipped, her stomach pressed against the bed, he proceeded to tie her wrists, then her feet, then each set of limbs to the bedpost. Her heart pounding under his palms, Paul could see the fire and fear in her eyes. He went to her kitchen, returning with a stack of ceramic plates, which he placed on her back, their meaning implied. Still silent, he left her bound in her bed as he set out to explore her house.

The kitchen was pristine, and Paul intended to keep it that way—after he had rifled through her food, of course. The hunt always made him hungry. He made himself a sandwich, began to re-twist the bread bag to seal it. *BATHUMP*. A sudden noise, not from the bedroom, but from the front porch, jolted him, causing him to drop the bread on the ground.

Traipsing carefully to the front door, Paul investigated. He peeked through the blinds carefully, opening them between his fingertips, revealing nothing outside to be worried about. Deciding that the noise was just a tree branch or animal, he returned to the kitchen.

Paul bent to pick up the discarded bread on the ground. *Not on my life*, he gestured at the bread, giving it the universal "I'm watching you" gesture. He'd always been so careful; misplaced footprints would not be the end of him.

Sandwich in hand, Paul made his way back to the bedroom. He chewed on his turkey and cheese, kneeling next to the bed to look into the eyes of the woman he'd soon kill. He smiled, mouth full of food, tomato in his teeth.

"Perfect," the first word he'd uttered to her. And the last she'd hear as he plunged his switchblade into the back of her neck. She died quickly, the smell of Paul's breath, ripe with meat and cheese, the last thing she'd process.

Paul worked the knife, eventually cutting away a thick square of skin which he cast aside onto one of the plates he'd brought in earlier. *Art*, he thought to himself, a grin on his face. *A cannibal's buffet.*

He wasn't a cannibal though, so took another bite of his sandwich as the blood pooled around her, staining her sheets. He could already imagine the crime scene photos, with their charismatic lighting making the blood look greasy as it settled into the mattress below, the dark center surrounded by the thinner washed red tint.

Bending over her again, he stuck his knife into her neck once more, severing tendons and nerves to eventually pry a single vertebra from her back. He held the piece of her spine in his hand, happy to have rested from her his token, leaving behind his signature.

Aroused at this moment, and ready to take it all in, Paul finished his sandwich and closed his eyes, sniffing and pulling the scent of sweat and tears and death to him. He caressed the dead woman's hair, when suddenly his own stood up on his neck as he heard from the front of the house the telltale sound of a door slowly opening. A light creaking noise.

He waited for footsteps, hearing none.

"You got ghosts or something?" he asked the corpse, laughing.

Following the same lack of logic as his victims, he ignored the feeling that he could potentially be dooming himself. It was his moment, and he intended to see it through.

Paul continued his routine, blaming his imagination for the false noises he was now sure he hadn't heard, plucking hair from the head of his victim. *Another prize for Spine Stalker.* He began to whistle, looking around the room, committing the bloodstain, the body, the look of death to his memory so he could replay the night between his next murders.

Shuffle. A pause. *Shuffle.* Now Paul knew what he heard. Gentle, careful footsteps in the front hall, tracing the steps he'd taken not long ago. Inside, Paul was screaming, clamoring to figure out what he should do, but his movements were stilled, frozen in place at the sounds and uninvited guest. He took two steps back, easing the bedroom door ajar before silently climbing behind it, back flush against the wall and forcing his sweat against his clothes.

Step. Step. Step. The footsteps grew closer, and Paul gripped his switchblade tighter in his hand. *She was supposed to be single!* his mind shouted at him, wondering how he could get this night so wrong when it had felt so right.

With the shuffling sounds right outside the door, Paul awaited the arrival. A woman stepped into view.

He expected her to make a sound, to acknowledge the bound and bloodied body before her, but she, like Paul, remained wordless. Paul could, however, see her sense him behind her, and as her head whipped around he was stunned.

"Rosie?" he said, relieved.

"Paul," she replied, eyes alight with excitement.

His gut burned. It was the knife inside that did it.

"Must be something in the air," she winked at him, before turning and walking away, leaving him to bleed out in his victim's room.

The press is going have a field day, he numbly thought to himself. He couldn't believe his bad luck, kicking himself for becoming Rosie's next victim. *She really doubled down on me.*

Paul rubbed his fingers across the vertebra still gripped in his hand, trying to enjoy the brittle bumps and sharp dips one last time. He could see the headline now. "Who stalked the Spine Stalker? Two dead at grisly scene," it would say. His face would be everywhere, but Rosie'd still have all the glory, and in this case, what was hers would truly be his as well.

Oh well. He drifted off, the blood pooling around him. *Beats losing your legacy to a bag of buns.*

Part Three: To Transform

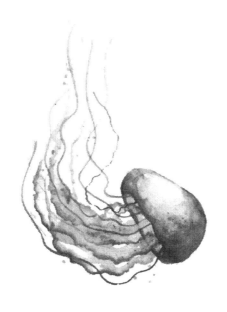

LIVE! FROM JEKYLL'S HIDEOUT

"Lights, camera, and... action!" The stage, lit with multi-colored spotlights, dazzled the audience, who began clapping as the first form came into view. A small figure made of cloth and wood stiffly walked from the castle door at the side of the stage. An arm raised and waved. The puppeteer, clad in a pageboy's cap, rested the child-like pawn on a shelf, facing the audience before walking from the shadows and into the spotlight. Dr. Jekyll came into view. He bowed, tipping his cap to the audience before taking his seat on the wooden tri-legged stool in the center of a beam of glowing green light.

His voice boomed with a warm, pleasant tone. "Welcome, families, friends! I'm so happy you could all be here tonight. I can't wait to share my favorite science stories and experiments with you all."

Jekyll smoothed his blue sweatshirt, the white collar of his dress shirt poking up to frame his neck. He looked out at the eager audience, twenty sets of eyes belonging to families from all around the country alight in anticipation.

"I have so many things to teach you tonight. A show to amaze, to astonish! For what?" he asked, holding his hands out to the audience.

"For Science!" a beautiful chorus of young and old voices yelled back.

The show began.

Jekyll stood up, walking to a sub-section of the stage. His set, built like a castle, displayed a small laboratory table with various instruments and substances spread across it, alongside a tower where he kept his props hidden behind a heavy oak door. He reached in and pulled out two life-sized puppets sewn together by a practiced hand. In one arm, a tall woman-puppet in a flowered blouse and denim jeans, and, cradled in the other, a smaller boy-puppet, a backwards hat on his head and glasses perched across his nose.

The puppets were anatomically proportioned, but their beady black eyes and fuzzy skin gave them away for what they were: cloth and filling, devoid of vitality.

"Well, folks, today we have Amanda and Ben here to help us learn about biomes." Jekyll propped the puppets up behind the laboratory table before pulling materials out of a wooden crate beneath.

He placed an empty two-liter on the table, filled it with dirt, and explained the process to the audience: "Biomes," he began, "consist of a community that works with the environment and each other to make their space habitable."

Jekyll pulled Ben's strings with calculated motions, forcing the doll boy's hands to pad the dirt down into a compact shape. "We have everything we need on this planet to continue to thrive, but sometimes we need help from each other and the natural resources and atmosphere on this planet. We live in symbiosis."

He placed a box in Amanda's hands, her palms outstretched with a few tugs of the puppet's pulley system.

"We started with the dirt." He tugged Jeremy's strings again, causing him to pat the dirt a few more times. The camera panned in close as Jekyll himself pinched a bit of the brown soil between his fingers, letting it fall back to the floor of the bottle. "Dirt—or more accurately, soil—is rich with nutrients. It can be made even more rich, however, by the flora and fauna in the biome."

He placed a few pieces of moss at the bottom. "Flora—plant-life," he explained.

He tugged Amanda's strings and she reached in the box she was holding. "And…" she pulled a few worms from the box and handed them to Jekyll. "Now, fauna," he continued. "Thank you, Amanda," he said to the puppet, earning laughter from the audience, along with a smaller array of "ewwww"s. He smiled, knowing he'd likely garner the same reaction from the children watching him from home.

Jekyll continued explaining the workings of the biome: how when you closed the cap off, poking a few holes for air, you created atmosphere, and eventually condensation. The plants would grow, the worms would digest refuse, and the biome could survive for quite some time, a little Earth among the greater Earth. Along the way, his puppets helped to point out interesting facts, hold his materials, serve as the butt of the occasional joke. The pulley system was a lot of work, but it was his gimmick and it looked great for camera close-ups. Jekyll was so grateful for their contribution to his grandest science experiment.

Or, perhaps, not his grandest, as *that* was lying on his laboratory table deep within his castle walls, waiting for the show to end. Jekyll hoped he'd secure his next volunteers from the crowd. He was ready to finish his prized experiment tonight.

Jekyll's mind twirled around the tantalizing prospects as he continued his on-stage demonstration. He was almost done when a small voice from the audience spoke up.

"But what if they die?" a small boy wearing a dinosaur t-shirt asked.

Jekyll grinned. "But what if what dies?"

The child squirmed, before answering. "The worms. Or the plants. Or the dirt."

"Ah, smart boy. Dirt can't truly die. It isn't alive." Jekyll replied, a kindness in his voice that always soothed the audience. "But, the plants, the worms... they might. However, when they do, they aren't without purpose. They still give nutrients to the dirt, to the biome, to help others grow and live."

The crowd was enthralled. They sat at the edge of their seats, backs straight like the teeth of a comb.

Jekyll continued, his time for that day's episode almost at its end. "We all grow and live. We all die." He looked straight at the camera. "But even in death," he paused dramatically, "we all have a purpose."

Silent, the audience inched forward in their seats, jumping as Jekyll yelled, "Cut!" and the cameras stopped filming, activated by his voice. The crowd clapped for the show's ending and began to form a line to meet Jekyll. On TV sets across the nation, the familiar closing song and credits would signal the end of another episode of *Jekyll's Hideout*.

Jekyll stood at the front of the stage, shaking hands and doling out colloquialisms, thanking the people for their attendance and for learning with him. At the end of the line, the boy in the dinosaur shirt who had asked the final question held his dad's hand, eyes glued to the floor. With the rest of the audience gone, the pair walked up to greet Jekyll.

"That was a great question you asked there. What's your name?"

The boy's father nudged the kid forward. "Seth," the kid said.

Jekyll bent down to shake his hand. "Well, Seth. You asked something that troubles us all but is an important reminder in life. Thank you for that."

"He's a smart kid. Tough to crack and always asking questions," Seth's father said.

"Just like me when I was a boy." Jekyll winked, then ran his hand along his beard. "Say, would you two like to see the inner workings behind the show? I can show you some of the behind-the-scenes rooms in *Jekyll's Hideout*."

Seth nodded, his head bobbling up and down. He looked up to his father, hoping to see approval.

"That sounds great," the father replied. "I'm Anthony, by the way."

"A pleasure to meet you both," Jekyll said. He walked towards the back door in the room. "Follow me."

The three walked out through the door and were met with a long, winding staircase. Jekyll took the lead, a hand on the ivory-colored banister. "I'll show you the experiment showcase room first."

Gliding up the stairs, Jekyll ushered the pair into a deep red room with various glass exhibits lining the walls. Bones, bugs, minerals, chemicals... the exhibits were plentiful and a visual feast of the macabre and scientific. "Here we have all of the experiments I've shown on my previous episodes."

Seth ran up to the first exhibit, eyes scanning the case. "This is so cool!" he exclaimed, pointing at a set of robotic hands that opened and closed a geode repeatedly.

Jekyll walked back towards the door. "I'll leave you two here for a few moments. I have to go make sure the servers got today's episode out. Take your time here; soak it all in. For what?" he asked.

"For Science!" Seth replied.

Jekyll left the room.

The true laboratory was not unlike the small table set up on the stage of *Jekyll's Hideout*, covered in beakers, tubes, wires, and cages of animals and plants baring teeth. Much more elaborate, with a sinister air about it, as Jekyll always had some novel idea for the advancement of science.

Jekyll wished he could expose his laboratory to the world; he yearned to change the maligned vision of science, so sterile and gray, and show people just how colorful and gorgeous it could be. The colors of the liquids in various jars and beakers glowed intensely, like jellyfish found in deep ocean waters. The plants were vibrant, their greens radiating emerald hues and their flowers unlike anything you'd find in a grocery store.

Science itself was beautiful, even if her methods were dark.

He saved the mystical, the bright, the simple for his shows. Seeing the smiles light up on children's faces as they delighted in education brought a pride to Jekyll's heart that was worth the world.

But what he kept for himself, behind laboratory doors, after the camera shuts off, *that* was his true purpose.

He fumbled through his tables, checking the vitals of the creatures on his slabs. Their heart monitors were steady in their peaks and repetition. They'd be ready soon.

First though, he needed a few more parts.

And before that, he needed his courage.

Facing the darkest parts of himself and his purpose, Jekyll poured a pint of a bright green liquid into a sturdy glass. *For Science*, he thought, and he downed the contents in three gulps.

The transformation was always slow to start. Dividing your soul into its best and worst halves takes time, takes focus on the universe's part. Rearranging a human is far from an effortless endeavor.

Jekyll's anger moved to the forefront. It was always the first thing he noticed, marking the change. His pent-up wrath exploding like bubbles from a shaken bottle of champagne. Popping.

The anger clouded the guilt, the sensation that what he was doing couldn't possibly be forgivable, even if it advanced knowledge. This was the sensation Jekyll was eager to have shouldered by his other half. His heart was kind, and he hated that his actions had consequences.

With relentless desires driving his thoughts, Jekyll's body shifted. His eyes widened, the brows moving upwards, stretching thin to accommodate the gleaming madness. His teeth grew, twisting from his gums like corkscrews, ready to rip into the world. Testosterone pumped through his veins, causing sprouts of hair to appear in patches across his body. His knees bowed, carrying the weight of his guilt. He looked every part to be a ghoul, but his strength belied his long, buckled frame.

Hyde had taken over, and he stormed back to the hallway.

Seth and Anthony were admiring a small tank filled with tarantulas when Hyde entered the room.

Seth turned toward the door to greet Jekyll. "Dr. Jekyll, I was wondering if you named—"

He screamed, taking in the monstrous form lurching toward him and his father. He looked like Dr. Jekyll, but Seth refused to believe that the kind educator could be this hideous, erratic creature.

At Seth's scream, Anthony turned around and was able to let out a "What the—" before a massive, gnarled fist clubbed him over the head. Anthony thumped to the ground in a heap, out cold.

Hyde swiveled and faced the boy. He grunted at the small child before grabbing him and hoisting him over his shoulder. With his other hand, he grabbed Anthony's boot-clad foot and dragged them from the room.

Anthony slid across the floor of the hallway, his shirt falling to his chest. Seth wiggled in Hyde's hairy arms, shrieking every other step, his face turning red as tears dripped from his cheeks.

"Stop," Hyde grunted, before kicking open the laboratory door. He placed the boy on the nearest slab, confining his limbs with cotton restraints secured to the table. Breathing heavily, Hyde dragged Anthony to the sterilizing shower and tossed him in. He stripped him of his clothes and turned the nozzles, releasing the disinfectant spray onto his skin. The unconscious man was powerless to stop the highly-pressurized streams from striking his skin like hundreds of needles.

Hyde turned on a camera, recording his steps so that Jekyll could later watch, unable to remember his dark counterpart's evil actions. Like the syndication of *Jekyll's Hideout* each week, the evening would be a one-man show.

Jekyll managed the entire production for his show, leaving no room for error or misplaced secrets. There were no cameramen, no gaffers, no light artists. Only Jekyll and his audience. His puppets. And then, at night, Hyde.

Tonight, there would be two more transformations. Hyde turned his attention to the struggling Seth, thrashing about the table, restrained by cotton-rimmed cuffs. Grabbing a mask attached to a tank of nitrous oxide, Hyde placed his meaty hand on Seth's chest. He affixed the mask over the boy's mouth and heard the whine of the gas canister letting loose its contents into Seth's lungs. Seth stopped beating his limbs against the table as the chemicals kicked in.

Hyde attached the sedated boy to a variety of tubes, sliding them under his skin and deep into muscles, nanofibers adhering to nerves. Hyde's thick, gnarled fingers flipped switches, and a barrage of neon liquids made their way under his skin and deeper into his veins. As minutes passed, the boy's skin parted at the pores, germinating sprouts of fibers. His blood turned to a dense cotton, veins rearranging into wires, burgeoning from his back at the shoulders, the nape of his neck, the tops of his thighs. His eyes rolled out of his head, and Hyde replaced them with black, shiny buttons.

Dead, then born anew. The cast of *Jekyll's Hideout* growing by one.

The puppet-boy screamed.

The newest iteration of the experiment—the addition of a voice for more lifelike ventriloquism for Jekyll's skits—had worked. The boy's mind fading at last, the screaming stopped. Hyde smiled.

Now, for the final new transformation of the night.

Hyde loped back to the shower, turned off the stream, and pulled Anthony to another sterile table. Taking from death, adding to life, his mansion a biome, all parts in symbiosis with one another. Bone-saw in hand, Hyde went to work.

Jekyll awoke the next day, feeling like himself once more. Gone was the rage, the narrow focus. He was, again, the kind-faced educator, ready to prepare his next show. But first, he wanted to check the progress of his more brutish half. He walked swiftly to his laboratory.

He watched the playback of the night, grimacing as Hyde dealt the fates he was too sensitive to take care of himself. He could bear the fruits of science, knowing the outcome, the betterment of knowledge, but he could not bear the means.

And I'll never have to again, he thought, pulling the curtains back on his grandest experiment.

On the table, the puzzle of a man blinked. Made of parts of different men, flesh tones lighter, then darker, sewn together with black cable, Jekyll thought him perfect.

He only needed to drink one last concoction and he'd be free of his guilt, his madness, for good. He could face his dualities as two men, symmetrical goals of advancing science at all costs in mind. Hyde, encased in the jigsaw-jointed body, would be free to perform the dark tasks by night, while Jekyll contrived his own lighter experiments, free to continue to carry out his sensational educational program by day.

One content, the other manic.

Jekyll and Hyde smiled.

For Science.

ON THE SAME WAVELENGTH

"107.1, right?" Art asked, leaning over the center console to program the radio number.

"I think… sounds about right. Can you hurry up?" Jill's terse voice cut through the van to the front seat. "The movie's already started."

Art and Jill had arrived at the Jazzy Inn Drive-In five minutes late. The old complex was barely running, with rundown signposts and faded marked stalls, but the horror-hungry crowd still flocked to the theater every weekend in October to catch the themed horror movie lineup. Three movies a night, curated by horror professionals. This weekend, everyone was packed in tight ready to enjoy "Panic! At the Drive-In," the weekend's installment of Satanic-based movies.

When Art and Jill pulled up to the ticket booth in their '83 Vanagon, they were arguing. They hadn't been able to make it to the theater all month, and they wanted things to be perfect for their planned escape from home life with the new baby. Just one night.

As Art passed the cashier their money, the staff member gave them directions in a hushed, brisk tone that could barely be heard over the bickering. "You'll just want to turn that radio dial to 101.7," he said, finger outstretched. "You might want to write that down… okay… still arguing… have a nice evening!" The heated couple waved their hands in a circle to say thanks and drove their car to their space at the back row of the parking lot.

While Art took care of the audio, Jill spread a frayed blanket across the trunk of the van, propped some lumpy pillows up behind the seats, and arranged a bowl of popcorn between the two. The argument had finally subsided, and Art flicked the station to 107.1. The dulcet tones and shrill shrieks of the movie score played through the minivan's speakers. There was a light popping sound, almost discernible, lost in the synthetic tones.

"You sure this is the right station?" Jill asked.

"Kid said 107.1. And the sound's coming through."

"Could have sworn it was something else," Jill mumbled. She shrugged inwardly, not wanting to strike up another heated debate.

The couple jumped in the back, sliding up to a comfortable position, letting out simultaneous sighs as they settled in to watch the movie.

The first movie was over quickly; a short runtime of an hour and fifteen minutes had caused a cacophony on the screen and in the thoughts of viewers. *Why was the demon in the basement hellbent on ruining the lives of teens? What a dud*, Art thought to himself.

"I heard the second movie has really been making waves," Jill said from her spot by Art's side. "Something about cults and brainwashing and all that jazz. I heard it's gimmicky too, like the old Castle films."

"As long as the gore's good, I'm satisfied," Art replied.

Jill rolled her eyes. "I hope you get your wish, sweetie. Good gore all around."

The movie began, and the couple was immediately enthralled. So enthralled that they didn't notice the slight sound differences between their car and their immediate neighbor's audio. The dialogue was unchanged, and the music hit the same beats, but every so often a parade of ticking could be heard from the speakers.

The opening scene was comprised of a group of dark figures circled around an unconscious male, stripped to his undergarments. The dark figures fritzed in and out of focus, blurring their forms repeatedly. *Whoa*, Art thought. *Haven't quite seen effects like that before.*

The men, clad in black robes, too-pale faces peering from under the hoods, surrounded the male, mumbling under their breath. A strange chanting began drifting over the radio.

"*Surge tenebras animarum*," the radio blared on top of a synth score. "*Intra corpus. Extra corpus.*" As the droning Latin continued, the ominous circle of men blinked in and out in front of the transfixed male's body. Each time their forms fizzle in the frame, a new piece of flesh was missing from the body of the man on the altar.

"*Surge tenebras animarum*," they continued, repeating the phrases again. Their voices were one, piercing the night in their succinct delivery.

Art began to feel strange, buzzing from head to toe, like his body had fallen asleep at some point. The audio sounded discordant, detached from the movie. The phrasing and cadence didn't seem to match the mouths moving on the screen, even with all their blinking in and out of focus. Art felt like he was watching an Italian exploitation film, famous for their style of dubbing.

A high-pitched squeal started in the base of Art's skull, moving to his forehead.

"Yikes. Massive headache," Art mumbled while rubbing his temples, trying to push the radiating pain away.

"Headache twins?" Jill replied, eyes wincing closed slightly.

"I hope you're not my sister…" Art playfully grinned, trying to forget the strange throb in his head.

"Hands to yourself!" Jill shrieked, eliciting a sharp "Shh!" from the car next to the couple. "Pay attention to the movie, you dork."

Art and Jill continued watching the captivating film. With every murder—and they were plentiful—the dark cloaked figures were blinking in and out of locations, wreaking havoc with their chants. Upon slaying every victim, they uttered the strange phrases, and pieces of the victim's skin began floating away in chunks, revealing the musculature underneath. Each time the phrases came across the radio, not quite synced with the video on the screen, Art and Jill's head throbbed evermore.

"My head is killing me," Art finally gave in. "You wanna head home?"

"Let's see it through. We've probably only got a little left."

The couple pushed to the final moments of the movie, filled with the most intensive chanting yet. "*SURGE TENEBRAS ANIMARUM!*" the figures shouted. The stereo in the car could hardly keep up with the volume of the chanting. "*INTRA CORPUS. EXTRA CORPUS.*"

The car started to shake from the thundering sounds and the neighboring vehicles' inhabitants began to stumble out of their cars and stare at Art and Jill's van.

Within the vehicle, a nightmare unfolded. Art sat up straight, mouth open, watching in frozen horror as Jill dissolved before his eyes. Just like the scenes they'd spent the last hour watching, Art and Jill were coming apart, piece by piece. New chunks of skin went missing with every passing second, blinking in and out of a visible spectrum.

Art stared ahead, stiff as a board and splintering like human wood, watching as fingers fell off. Jill was missing most of her torso, the flesh stripped from her neck up to her chin.

If they were screaming, they couldn't be heard above the sharp static cutting through the air.

They weren't the only affected vehicle—several other cars throughout the lot were blinking in tandem with the movie and the chanting, their inhabitants disappearing inside only to reappear moments later, coming undone.

Groups of people throughout the parking lot congregated around the handful of vehicles that were pulsating with the screaming chants. Their questions grew louder and more frantic.

"Why is the volume so loud?"

"This doesn't sound like the movie."

"Who's chanting?"

"Oh God!"

As the movie-goers panicked, the vehicles with the chanting audio over station 107.1 began to blink in and out, dark shadows circling around the cars. The passengers inside continued to fall apart, piece by piece, in a bloody, disassembled mess.

With one final whispered "*Surge tenebras animarum*", the credits rolled. Some applauded, some screamed. The gore was good, the gimmick fulfilled, and the radio dials swiftly switched to 101.7, leaving no trace of the dangerous wavelengths that had infected Art, Jill, and ten other movie-goers who lay still, an incomplete shell of the people they once were.

Their bodies—or what was left of them—were taken away. Cars moved to dusty lots, property bound by chains. The incident at the Jazzy Inn Drive-In was the end for the victims, a dozen in total, as far as the rest of the world was concerned.

But for those that the nightmarish radio waves destroyed, it was only the beginning.

Art and Jill were just bits of meat on a cement ground, a lightbulb flickering overhead. On, off, on, off. Staying off. Darkness.

The flesh was ragged, torn at the edges. The bits that were Art and Jill were not alone, surrounded by the fragments of skin, muscles, and whites of bone that had been the other doomed movie-goers. Their company had shared a ride on that volatile frequency that not only ripped their bodies apart, but transported them—a version of them, at the very least—to somewhere vacant, desolate.

Dry air withered their pieces.

The lightbulb fluttered back on,

The lumps of twelve people, glued to the ground. The ability to move was stripped from their being, but their ability to think…

Art was all too aware of his vulnerability, that pieces of his hands were stuck amongst parts of his wife's leg, mingled with strangers. He couldn't talk, couldn't scream, could only feel the void of infinite nondescript pain, the phantom attachment between chunks.

He wished to pull himself together, but scattered, he remained.

One of Art's dispersed ears picked up a sound. Echoing footsteps, multiple, heading his way. An eyeball that sat atop a flap of his wife's abdomen watched as a group of figures entered the room.

Their black cloaks were dusty and ripped, frayed at the edges. Hoods hung low over pale faces. Art recognized them as the monks from the movie, something he remembered watching what felt like decades ago.

The monks circled the piles of flesh, sprinkled across the ground like leaves on a windy autumn day. They didn't speak—didn't need to in the void where this scene existed, trapped between frequencies somewhere on a wavelength.

Two robed men carrying wire brooms approached the broken bodies. They swept, pushing the chunks to the center of the room, making a pile of meat. Art marveled at how big the pile grew, losing parts of himself in the conglomeration of the viscera of the lost people.

Once the flesh was collected, more men carrying buckets filled the room. The monks bent low to the ground, scooped the human-pile into their hands, and deposited the pieces into the bins. The torn bits made soft and heavy thumps as they hit the metal container.

The buckets full, the monks lifted the containers, their shoulders sagging under the weight of the separated portions of a dozen adult humans. They walked, caring not who the people were, only that they had enough sustenance to satisfy their Honor, lord of the dimension in which they existed.

One foot in front of another dragged forward, robes tangling in the wind whooshing through the shafts of the underground palace.

From within a bucket, Art cried, an eye pushing a tear onto the arm of someone else, letting his sadness wash across their skin undisturbed. His nose, carried in a bucket five paces ahead, caught a sickly scent in the air, smelling like the candied breath of a dying man.

The robed men continued forward, sandaled feet walking atop the concrete, gray floor patterned with bloody footprints, in directions both to and from their destination.

They'd done this before, but never with a bounty as big as this one

A joyous rumble of a laugh echoed from across the room as the monks entered, buckets clanging against their legs as the exertion of the journey weakened their arms.

Atop a throne built from steel, the edges sharpened like razors, sat a giant of a man. His height loomed over the monks standing before him, towering over them even from his sitting position. His muscles rippled beneath his black robe. He was bald, eyes black, but buzzing intermittently with static. His teeth were curved and sharp.

The lips of a thousand faces puckered across his body, mouths open in silent screams

The men bowed, presenting the buckets to their Honor who grinned a ghastly, bloody smile. He motioned wordlessly to them, and they used their hands to ladle the collected flesh into his gaping maw.

He swallowed, the meat visibly crawling down his throat. He feasted.

With every bite, his stomach grew. As the contents of the buckets dwindled and joined the refuse in his gut, new faces emerged on the Honor's body.

On his chest, Jill. Above his eyebrow, Art.

With the newly sacrificed settled into their new homes, a buzzing filled the room. The mouths opened, and a droning noise joined the high-pitched reverberations.

The Honor raised his arms, face alight with his blood-grin, conducting life and death on his personal wavelength.

THE SLOW SIEGE OF ZENOHTOWN

Kyla drove her clunked-up beater of a car—mired by rust, with a missing headlight and barely-sputtering parts under the hood—to an oasis of a town. She glanced at the postcard, clipped to the passenger side visor. *Dive into Zenoh Lake!* the postcard boasted. *Shimmer With Us!* begged the bottom of the card, spread in a bombastic font across a picture of an eerily blue-green lake.

Most people wouldn't understand her nomadic life, her ability to go from place to place, doing odds and ends of work at each location, making just enough money to get her to the next destination. She'd left the last city with enough money in her pocket after doing some delivery work that she had felt comfortable in this last leg to take her time. She felt she knew Zenohtown as soon as she'd heard the first rumbling of it. She couldn't remember where she'd heard the name, it felt like it just appeared in her mind. As soon as she heard it, she'd dug into the glove compartment of her car to pull out a dog-eared map, seeing the name only a couple hundred miles from her current spot. So, on she drove.

Her car clambered up the hill, crested the foreign terrain, passed the *Welcome to Zenohtown, population 5016* sign, pulled into a diner lot, and died on the spot. The lot was filled with cars of all makes and models and years and conditions and rich design and poor design and garish colors and practical colors—but all very, very dead.

With her car broken down and showing no signs of turning back on, Kyla walked into the diner and was greeted by the smiling faces of the gentle folk enjoying a meal by the light of the early afternoon. The old woman wiping a cloth over the counter in front of her smiled extra bright.

"Hello there, darlin'," she cooed, with an accent that didn't quite sound southern, but still had the charm and softness. She continued, smiling warmly: "Welcome. Haven't seen you in here before. What can I getcha?"

Kyla's stomach rumbled, though she wished she wasn't hungry. She was far more concerned about her broken-down car in the parking lot, along with the abundance of other broken-down cars spread about in the vicinity.

"Thanks…"—she looked at the waitress' nametag— "…Lisa. First time out here, and thought the town sounded nice. Wanted to check it out to see if it was a good place, but my car stalled out back there. Any good mechanics around? Anyone I could call out to?"

"Oh, don't you worry about that. Zenohtown's been known to make a few cars… immobile once they cross her threshold. Why don't I get you some nice soup for now, and we'll figure out that car of yours?" Lisa said.

Kyla considered her options, which were looking like exactly one, and resolutely took her seat. "Soup sounds great. Any kind, I'm not picky and would love a recommendation."

Lisa smiled widely. "Sure thing, Kyla. Let's get you some of that good soup."

She knew Kyla's name. But before Kyla could question it, Lisa had dashed off to the back, leaving Kyla at the counter, surrounded by strangers who would become routinely less strange over the next few hours. Kyla checked her phone—dead, too—and hoped that her journey to Zenohtown wasn't the worst mistake of her life.

Jasmine, Ralph, Sally, and Stu all piled in the cab of Sally's daddy's big blue pickup truck and vowed to ride east and stop at the first town they came across. They puttered along, windows down, feeling in love with each other and their lot in life, swearing one last adventure until the four parted ways for college at summer's end.

They'd driven miles, hundreds of them, along long hilly routes in between wide stretches of desert land. They could see the vague outline of a town in the distance, and signs pointing to civilization. "Zenohtown" the signs proclaimed, home to a shimmering lake, hiking, hot springs, and desert riding. The friends hadn't bothered to check a map; they just wanted to drive as far as the roads could take them. But had they looked, they'd have found Zenohtown to be a one-route-in and one-route-out kind of place, nothing but a small blip in a big backcountry terrain, and would have opted to stay elsewhere. All things considered, that would have been the better decision. But decision-making was not their strong suit.

Stu slammed his meaty hand into Ralph's back, causing Ralph to turn the steering wheel in a direction opposite of his intended path. The truck swerved, then righted itself.

"What the hell, man?!" Ralph shouted.

"My bad, my bad," Stu replied, hands in the air. "I'm just so pumped that we are going to take these babies out to the desert here, and get some real riding in." He pointed his thick thumb in the direction of the bikes tethered to the truck's bed.

"If you wanted to ride us, you didn't have to take us all the way out to shithole nowhere." Sally smirked, her blonde head shining by the light of the setting sun.

It was Jasmine's turn to do some smacking as she swatted at Sally's leg. "Oh gross, no. I agreed to come on this trip for the fun, and *that* kind of riding would go against that plan."

"Hey!" both boys protested in unison.

The four laughed together, one of the last good laughs they'd get, as the truck rumbled to a stop near a sign that advertised "Camping Permitted" with a picture of a blue tent smeared across aging wood. The campsite was nestled just on the outskirts of town, barely off the road, and the four were unbothered as they recognized the solitude of the place. There'd be so few cars passing by that they could leave their truck, belongings strewn about with no concern of stolen goods. Who'd know?

Deciding to take their motorbikes to the lake, no matter how far the journey, the group began gearing up and removing the bikes from the back of the truck.

A thousand eyes watched from the sand around them. Who'd know? *They'd know*.

Kyla had just finished her lunch, scraping the sides of the bowl to get every last fleck of the split pea soup with chunks of ham into her stomach. No matter how unappetizing split pea soup looked, it was always such a treat: salty and creamy, especially with the ham grazing her tongue. The soup from the diner tasted even better, spiced with something she'd never quite tried before, creating a delightful warmth in her stomach. She hoped it was a taste of what was to come in Zenohtown.

With her belly full, Kyla looked around the lively diner. People of all ages and backgrounds were huddled in booths, forking food into their mouths at a fast clip, smiling, laughing, exchanging stories. Kyla couldn't help but feel longing, aching to be able to fit in like the people here, mostly because she'd been told she belonged nowhere else. Not in the rural west, surprisingly conservative (too gay); or the Midwest, less-surprisingly conservative (too brown). And she chose to avoid the big cities (too loud, too expensive, too much).

She began to think that her car breaking down in the parking lot was a sign, something to be celebrated rather than felt as a burden. Who needed a car if one never planned on leaving? *Maybe*, Kyla thought to herself, looking around at the cheerful residents, *longing can finally become belonging*.

She continued watching the movements of the other diner guests, and while she was welcomed by their chumminess, she couldn't help but notice something... off. Something about their mannerisms felt forced, loud, too... synchronized. Like mimes telling a story that had no substance, only feeling.

"Okay to take?" Lisa gestured to the incredibly empty bowl in front of Kyla, breaking her thoughts.

"You bet," Kyla responded. "It was delicious! Hit the spot after the long drive."

Lisa smiled with a knowing look in her eyes. "It always does."

"Can I get the check?" Kyla asked.

"No, sweetie. This one's on us. A little welcome to Zenohtown from us all." Lisa's smile continued. The never-ending grin would have creeped her out on anyone else's face, but Kyla found it reassuring, especially in her current state of displacement.

"Thank you," Kyla said. "Well, since my car's probably gonna be stuck there for a while, where do you suggest a stranger head to?"

"Zenoh Lake is really beautiful this time of year. You can see all sorts of things living inside it and the water is really out of this world. Shimmers just like the stars above! Feels like home," Lisa enthusiastically answered.

"That sounds lovely!" Kyla beamed.

"And, if you've got a swimsuit, there's some hot springs right down the road from there to relax for the rest of the evening," Lisa continued.

"Excellent. I'll try and pop into a shop to get one and then head up there," Kyla said. "What about a place to stay for the night?"

"Or couple of nights." Lisa winked. "Or forever!"

"Ha, let's start with a couple and see how that goes. Gotta lay down roots somewhere, but who knows if this is the place? It's been a long time since I've had a home," Kyla said, quietly.

"Zenohtown will lay its roots in you. And that's a promise." Lisa placed a soft hand on Kyla's. "But, if you're looking for a place for the night, there's an inn up the road. The Bread and Breakfast. Best morning delights you'll find."

"Thank you, again, for the soup," Kyla said. "And the information. I'm sure I'll be back in soon. It was really nice to meet you."

"Nice to meet you too, honey. We're sure you won't be a stranger," Lisa said.

Kyla purchased a swimsuit from the shop next door to the diner, a perfectly cut navy one-piece. She loved the way it brought out the richness of her dark skin tone and couldn't wait to dip into the hot spring Lisa had mentioned. She'd asked directions while in the shop and was thrilled to hear it was only a mile away. It would be a nice little jaunt through the town, and she vowed to keep an open mind at the possibility of staying in the oddly pleasant place.

As she walked up the winding dirt path into the woods where the lake promised to be, that thought was on repeat. It was beautiful here, the contrast of the desert with the thick wooded area something not often seen. All around her, she felt a presence, something warm and welcoming, beckoning her further within. She wasn't threatened by it, but rather felt a burst of excited exploration coming her way.

Kyla worked out the path in her head. She'd hit up the hot springs first, resting her weary back in the soothing water, and then try to catch the lake as the sun set. She wondered if it would look as beautiful in person as it did on the postcard. Walking on, she followed the foliage-laden path deeper into the woods, the trees engulfing her. The wind picked up and shook leaves above her, and unbeknownst to Kyla, a hundred tiny organisms rained down on her head.

Ralph and Jasmine zoomed forward on their bikes, kicking up a trail of dust behind them. They could see the tree line in front of them and could hear the whirring of their friends' bikes behind them. They raced on, trying to beat the sun and get to the lake where they couldn't wait to sink their bodies.

The wind whipped around them, their helmets shielding their eyes from the chunks of dirt and rocks being kicked up. They felt like gods on those bikes, together enjoying the slow burn of summer, their friendship, and the memories they were making.

The eyes around the pack of friends were envious, resentful of their arrival. Every visitor had a different fate. Some they would take. Others, they would destroy. And these four, they were ripe for absorption. Zenohs had quite the way of making Earth their own.

The lake, thelakethelakethelake, the lake, they whispered internally to one another.

The four friends were nearly there.

Kyla sighed in happiness, dipping her feet into the hot spring. She'd arrived to find the site empty, so she changed into her newly-purchased bathing suit and tested the water. She'd never actually been in a hot spring before, but she could tell by the warmth of the water that she would love it.

She eased her legs into the water, sinking her body up to her torso and felt around to find a place to sit. She found a rock with a flat surface and down she set her body, the heat feeling like a massage all over. She smiled, feeling truly at peace for the first time in a long time.

That peace didn't last long.

While Kyla had never experienced a hot spring before, she was pretty sure she wasn't supposed to feel what felt like thousands of legs crawling up her body, invisible spiders making their way to find a place to enter. Kyla immediately panicked, hating the creeping sensation, but loathing even more that she couldn't find their source.

She sprang from the spring, crying out, trying to determine what caused the feeling of cobwebs slung across her body. There was nothing there to shake off, to bat at, just an all-over tingling that felt like waking up on top of an anthill. She felt the legs everywhere: tickling her toes, surrounding her torso, lunging up her neck, and finally, submerging themselves in her ears.

As soon as it had started, it stopped. Kyla couldn't remember why she was outside of the hot spring and tiptoed back into the water, reclaiming her empty seat.

Just a few more minutes, she thought. *Just a few more minutes and then I'll check out the lake.* And there she sat, enjoying the warmth, oblivious to the notion that it no longer only came from the sultry water around her, but also from just below the surface of her skin.

Moments later, *they* had settled, binding to Kyla, becoming Kyla, belonging to Kyla. She heard the gentle tones, not out loud, but deep within. *The lake, thelakethelake, thelake* they said. And so, she followed.

With the lake in view, Kyla heard a yelled "Tally-ho!" as Stu brought his knees to his chest before splashing into the blue-green lake. The other three quickly followed suit, stripped down to their undergarments, flashes of flesh urging on the invisible eyes around them. Silent whispers continued their chant: *hereherehereherehere.*

The four sloshed about, enjoying the tepid water on their hot, dusty skin. They were picture-perfect, young adults enjoying vacation time, smiling and horsing around. They belonged on a postcard.

A postcard.

Kyla reminisced, taking in the lake that, for once, really did capture the true beauty of the location it advertised. As Kyla walked to the trees surrounding the lake, she saw the four friends and envied their freeness with one another. They belonged together, always having companionship, something Kyla yearned for her entire life. Happy, carefree.

The whispering around Kyla turned into an unheard scream. She felt the power, the movement of thousands of organisms. They pushed her forward, emerging from the trees, showing her that she needed to see, to watch as they absorbed. The group of friends began to panic as the water around them churned, blended by the small limbs of the invisible creatures.

Kyla's attention was glued to Stu. She could tell he couldn't see the dozens of thick legs whipping around him, finding purchase on his skin. He couldn't see them, but *god he could feel them* and it wasn't more than a few seconds later that the others felt them breach their skin too. The translucent legs climbed and searched and burrowed, making holes, entering holes, doing everything they could to get inside. It was agonizing, like hundreds of fiery pinpricks that exploded into rupturing flesh.

The group of friends couldn't see what was destroying them, one cell at a time, but having become partially-assimilated with the unseen population of Zenohtown, Kyla could. From her place at the lake's shore, she could make out the pinkish yellow-colored organisms, could see that they were roughly two inches in length. Tiny whips jutted from multiple sides of their soft, rubbery bodies, spinning and slapping at the surfaces of the trespassers' limbs. Their mouths—*plural*, Kyla noted—sucked at the water-flecked skin, creating new pores through which they entered. With a doorway opened, they all rushed in.

Stu and Ralph bellowed, feeling the organisms crawling into their bodies by any means necessary. Some forced entry through their skin, creating bloody holes in their wake, while others climbed up and through their urethras, compelling the tunnels wider. Jasmine and Sally fared no better, blood tainting the blue-green water around them as the organisms they couldn't see, couldn't defend against, swam from the lake and into their bodies, swirling in their guts, through their veins, trapezing off bones.

Kyla was unnerved, trapped somewhere between the terrifying intake of the horrific experience she was watching and a calming hum provided by the organisms inside her. She couldn't move, couldn't think, could only watch.

The group of friends continued to suffer. The organisms were no longer visible outside, having all found their way to the inner parts. Ralph had managed to climb to shore, while the other three were slowly being reduced to a mass of bubbling blood, looking nothing short of the aftermath of a shark attack in a B-movie. Much as the low budget films couldn't afford to show the actual eating, Jasmine, Sally, and Stu were diminished to pieces of themselves, gently exploding underwater into a cloud of bloody, satiated organisms, swimming back to their homes beneath the surface of the lake.

Ralph, however, was dissolving in full view, and Kyla could only watch, wide-eyed, as the destruction took place. His skin—or what was left beyond the horde of holes he'd amassed—bulged at the presence of the organisms. His eyes bugged, his cheeks ballooning, his entire body expanding beyond its limits before finally bursting. The organisms skittered away, having had their fill, and his aerosolized blood and bits of bones flew through the air, feeding the surrounding organisms who had not partaken in the initial attack.

Nothing was wasted in Zenohtown.

With the feast complete, Kyla felt the presence of the organisms within her diminish. She regained control of her limbs and her mind, unsure of how to proceed.

After several moments of indecisiveness, she settled on returning to town. She wasn't sure what she'd just witnessed, but she knew she needed to figure out a way to get out of there before those organisms did to her what they did to those poor kids.

They kept quiet beneath her skin.

Kyla made it back to town, walking the mile briskly, still wearing her one-piece bathing suit. The night had begun to settle in, a chill creating goosebumps across her flesh. The gentle glow of the lights on buildings got closer, and she turned her walk into a jog, closing the distance.

Before long, Kyla burst through the doors of the diner. The room was still filled with people in booths, all smiling from ear to ear. She panted, out of breath, hands on knees, searching for a familiar face, finally settling on Lisa's.

"You okay there, dear?" Lisa asked, wiping a dish in her hand with a food-stained towel.

"They're dead!" Kyla shouted, unsure of how to explain.

"Who's dead?" Lisa implored.

"These kids! At the lake. They… I don't know. They exploded… these creatures…" She trailed off, realizing how crazy she sounded trying to explain.

"No worries, honey," Lisa said, her platitudes starting to annoy Kyla. "That's just us."

Kyla balked, not comprehending what she meant. "Us? Look, Lisa, I just saw four kids get killed. Is there a sheriff around here? Someone I can call?"

"We know," Lisa continued. "We saw it too. We see everything."

Kyla was frozen once again, this time the confusing words keeping her in place. "I don't know what you mean. This is insane. If you saw what I saw you'd be calling an ambulance." She paused. "Okay, maybe not an ambulance, there's nothing left to really... revive. But someone! Those things have to be stopped!"

"Oh, Kyla." A menacing smirk crept across Lisa's face. "We've laid our roots here for so long now, making a nice home away from home," she said, pointing upwards. "We didn't ask for those kids, but we did ask for you." The movement in the diner stopped as the residents of Zenohtown turned their heads in a single fluid motion to face Kyla.

Kyla's heart fluttered, recalling the gentle pull she'd felt that had brought her to Zenohtown. Lisa stepped forward, closer to Kyla. "We want you. We *have* you. And we're ready for more. And we..."

Kyla backed away from the encroaching woman, whose face had begun to slough off.

"...we can't be stopped," she said, her tone distorting into a choir of voices.

Kyla yelped as Lisa and the other diners began to dissolve. They didn't explode like the teens at the lake, but they became undone, breaking down into smaller pieces, diffusing into the small organisms Kyla recognized from the lake. The diner filled with a mass of tiny limbs, mouths, and fleshy parts, flagellating their way through the diner towards Kyla.

Kyla ran.

Her feet beat pavement once out of the diner, past her broken car amongst the dozens of others in the parking lot. The cars, Kyla now understood, were not unlike their missing owners—all makes and models and years and conditions and rich design and poor design and practical colors and garish colors but all very, very dead. The difference, however, being that the owners had left the cars for dead, and the true residents of Zenohtown had *made* the owners dead.

She ran, right out of Zenohtown, down the long road she'd driven in on. The organisms weren't giving chase, but Kyla couldn't care less.

In the distance, Kyla saw a blue pickup, devoid of passengers. She ran to the car, feeling relief flood her as she saw keys behind the visor of the passenger seat.

She jumped in the car, skin crawling at the thought of those organisms catching up to her. Her trembling hand inserted the keys into the ignition. Huffing from the exertion of her escape, she drove out of Zenohtown, no destination in mind, just as far away as possible.

Maybe the city, she thought. And from within, a hundred minds agreed. *The city, thecitythecity.* Yes, they'd like the city.

TINY DOG, BIG BITE

See? There she is again. I'm trying to take my thrice-daily walk, watering lawns, taking in the flowers, saying hi to the others, and there's Arla, speed-walking around the complex, phone in hand ready to call the apartment manager if anything looks out of place.

I narrow my eyes at her, seeing the sun glint off her stupid silver cat brooch, then wiggle my hind legs and tug on the leash. Time to go, Royce, you old git. His white, tucked-in tank top and gym shorts do him no favors. You'd think with all the walking we do he'd lose a little weight, but his gut's jutting out from the too-many beers he's been consuming that complement his Hungry Man diet. Let's gooooo.

We walk around the square complex a few times. I growl at the dogs that aren't part of my pack and amicably sniff and play with the ones that are. There're the chihuahuas down the street, Pico and his brother Gallo—they're good people. They usually know the best places to hang out when the moon comes around, high and proud. I've got a mad crush on Dizzie, the tiny Pomeranian across the way. And then, there's mean ol' York, the Yorkie.

We're a good pack. We hunt, we hide. We keep the normal humans happy for the companionship we provide, and they treat us like gods. Maybe we are. Gods of this complex, at least.

Royce and I get back to our unit. Once inside, I'm off the leash and I take myself to the kitchen. The snacks are all snout level, and I nudge one off the shelf for Royce to open. He obeys, and soon the wonderful flavor of pork rinds coats my mouth. I eat a couple, almost immediately full. Royce could learn from my portioning.

I glance over at the calendar.

The end of the month is here, and with this one brings the moon. I yip in excitement, giving Royce my best prancy toes. My nails clack against the floor, and he lifts me up, holding me close.

"Who's a good boy that's going hunting tonight? Who is he?" Royce rumbles against my chest. I pant, lick his face, because the good boy is me.

I spend the rest of the day meandering about the apartment, going on my second walk, conferring with my pack and planning for the night. It's a no-brainer who's getting evicted this month. Poor Arla, I wish I could say we hardly knew ya.

I place my paws on the windowsill. The moon is glowing, about to reach peak placement in the sky. The time draws near.

I trot to the extra room, clear except for the tarp in the center. I lay in the middle, placing my head on top of my paws. I close my eyes and wait to feel the first moonbeams on my fur.

The light hits, and the transformation begins. If you think a human man turning into a wolf is bad, all elongation and sprouting fur and cracking bones, reverting to a human body after living as a small, yipping dog for thirty days is really something. I feel my tendons, my muscles growing after being compressed into tiny spaces for so long. It simultaneously feels like the best stretch of your life and the worst parts of waking-up-from-numb pins and needles.

My fur sucks back into my body, leaving a fine layer of hair behind. Longer hair sprouts from my head, a dark brown mess on top of a face that becomes more human by the minute as my snub nose pushes out from my face, sloping sharply. Claws become fingernails and toenails, and my dew claws recede.

Covered in a fine sheen of sticky sweat, I'm my normal six-foot height, naked, shivering, and ready to hunt.

Pico and Gallo are already at the meeting place beneath the basketball hoop in the corner of the complex. In their human form they were Pete and Greg, and they specialized in IT and computer services. We spend so much time as dogs nowadays, our old careers are as good as gone. It wasn't always like this. We used to be able to avoid detection, but once Ripper got caught in his wolf form, we knew things had to change.

Too many people with too many cameras in their hands. Too many people out looking for the strange, looking for us. It's much easier to hide a normal human murder than it is a series of wolf-mauled corpses, you know?

So, we changed tactics. Dogs instead of wolves, and tiny dogs at that. More dog than human as we pushed our transformations out further and further until the order of the moon had reversed. Suckered some lonely men into becoming our companions (though they'd really grown on us over time. Man's best friend and all that).

My attention turns to the form sauntering our way. Dizzie walks up, in a simple pair of jeans and an oversized sweatshirt. I understand her instinct to cover up. Once you spend most of your time coated in fur, it feels weird to have the breeze on your skin. Everything is so much colder.

She sidles up next to me, enjoying my body that's no longer that of a pug, dripping drool.

"How you doing, Chip?" she asks.

I shuffle my feet. "Enjoying the moon. Antsy. Ready." She snuggles into my arms and nods.

York arrives last. He's a thick guy, with a wide neck and the same off-putting underbite and greasy hair he wears in his dog form. He doesn't talk much as a man, which doesn't jive with his normally yappy disposition. I think maybe he enjoys being pretty, finding confidence in his long-haired form. They say true strength comes from the inside, but we just like him for his brute strength that comes in handy with some of our feistier prey.

"Do we even need to discuss who we're evicting this month?" I say.

"We're all thinking it, right?" Dizzie asks.

Pico and Gallo nod their heads, and at the same time say, "Arla."

York grunts in response.

"She's gotta go. One of these days, she's going to see us change," I offer.

"And her meat will last us the month, for sure," Dizzie says.

"See? Look at her." Gallo points down the lane. We can all see the shine of her phone's flashlight, creeping around apartment entryways, snapping photos of license plates on cars that are parked in the wrong spaces.

"She's got it coming," Pico agrees. We hear her sigh as she marks down another license plate of a car parked slightly over the lines.

"Really cleaning up this complex, one misplaced wheel at a time," Dizzie says.

"She probably should have started with us," I say. "The real scourges." I wink.

"Hungry," York mumbles, growling.

"Let's give it a little more time," I say.

The group agrees, and we move our meeting to a park nearby, not wanting to arouse Arla's suspicion before we're ready.

At the park, we all enjoy our time on two legs. It's not so much that we miss the things we can't do as dogs, more so that we miss the way things just feel. For example, dogs can't hold hands—at least not conveniently—so I treasure the time I can hold Dizzie's soft hand in mine, rubbing my fingers over knuckles.

Each month, Dizzie and I talk, enjoying the easy silences. The world feels much slower when you're standing upright.

Pico and Gallo are happy just to play tag and throw balls at each other, expending their never-ending energy. And York... York sits. He isn't quite twiddling his thumbs, but I couldn't tell you what's going on in that head except the passing of minutes.

Our group came together like all good groups do, over time, in serendipitous ways. I'd found Royce at the adoption agency. I picked him, tugging at his heart with my puppy eyes, hoping he'd take me as his. The first change by the light of the moon caught him by surprise, but at that point, he was all in. It was like that for all of us with our handlers.

I found Dizzie and invited her to join me. Told her about the lonely man in the neighboring unit. She scratched at his door, and he didn't think twice before scooping her up, claiming the beautiful Pomeranian as his own. Dizzie has a way about her that makes you love her.

Pico and Gallo were roaming a barren grocery parking lot. They were taken in by an old man who had a lot of love to offer. Dizzie and I eventually found them while on one of our monthly excursions and got their owner to move into our complex, keeping the family together.

York was an accident—a useful one, though. As a human, he lived with his partner, two doors down. He swatted at me, and I bit him in a fit of rage and gave him my gift. I don't think much changed in his relationship with his partner. Still gruff, just cuter. His quiet nature grew on us in the later months; it was easy to see how he balanced the pack.

Those happenstances. Those tugging feelings that pulled us alike things together. And then, pulled our handlers to us. It doesn't take much convincing to give lonely men something to love. A loyalty that remained unbroken, not at all swayed by some... light murder once a month.

Dizzie and I talk, Pico and Gallo run themselves ragged, and York sits. For hours, we enjoy it all.

An owl hoots in the distance, signaling the moving night. I pull out my knife, ready to get the ball rolling to get my pack fed.

"All right, that's our cue."

As one, we head back to the complex.

We aren't surprised to see Arla still on the prowl. She's the most tenacious busybody I've ever met, and I almost hate to kill her for it.

Our pack moves with the wind, approaching Arla from all sides. I don't think she can run far, but we want to move fast before our other neighbors are awoken by the noise. We always do a quick snatch and grab, bring them back to my apartment and slaughter them in the extra room. The meat gets stored in the freezer, and we are usually able to portion out the body over the month between the five of us. Arla's a bit on the tiny side, but she'll last just fine.

We all step in closer.

My mouth waters as I recall the taste of a fresh kill. In our canine form, as tiny as we are, we can subsist on dog food and human snacks, but nothing comes close to the satisfaction of human flesh. Even though we've evolved over time, shifting our dispositions to more easily stay undetected, we still crave the kind of meat you can't buy in a pet store.

Arla has her head buried in the dumpster area, looking for prowlers or misplaced garbage to report. She doesn't see us approaching from the walled-off sides, blocking her exits. She put herself in cover, and I thank the moon for our luck.

York pounces first. If he can do this clean, it makes our life easier. No blood out here to scrub later. Damn true crime enthusiasts out there know how to spot a bloodstain from a mile away these days.

York wraps his thick arms around Arla's body, putting her in a sleeper hold. Eventually, she sleeps.

"Well, that was easy," Pico remarks.

"Don't say it," Dizzie says.

"Almost… too easy," Gallo finishes.

York hoists Arla over his shoulders, and we walk towards my apartment. I can smell her, and the thought of meat makes me almost drool. The dull slapping sounds of her hands on York's back make it worse. I wipe my mouth. So much for almost. Damn you, Pavlov.

We open the door. Royce is sitting in the living room, surrounded by the other handlers for our crew, all older men, all seeking affection, all kinds of must-love-dogs. The extra stuff they get for their homes each month after cleaning out our prey's apartment is a bonus. Way too easy to make it look like someone just up and left in the middle of the night. Especially in this neighborhood.

Royce clears his throat, then pushes his glasses up his nose, turning the page of his book.

"I really enjoyed what the author did on page one seventy-five. Hiding the punch and then delivering it out of nowhere. Completely changed the story," Royce says. Bald heads around him bob up and down. They love their book club, held monthly on the night of the full moon. The perfect cover for our comings and goings and strange faces in the complex.

Royce nods in my direction, and the five of us go to the extra room, bringing Arla with us.

We shackle her in the corner, binding her mouth as well.

Arla's awake.

She's confused at first, her eyes clouded as she takes in her surroundings. It doesn't take long before confusion shifts to anger. We can see she's spitting mad, though she can't actually spit with the gag over her mouth. She's thrashing against her chains.

Dizzie rearranges the tarp at the center of the room, making sure it's not too kinked up. Easier to catch the blood if there's no surprise folds.

The night is almost gone. I can see the gentle hues of the sun rising in the distance. We have to act quickly. I turn my head to Pico and Gallo, who grab the struggling Arla and place her in the center of the tarp.

We work in silence; no need to explain anything to our prey. She knows she's going to die. Pico and Gallo hold her down by her arms. York holds her legs. I hand Dizzie my knife. She kneels next to Arla, who is screeching behind her gag. The moon dips lower.

I feel my transformation start, the others whining as they toil to keep theirs at bay just a few minutes longer. My limbs shorten, fur sprouts, my teeth sharpen. My face wrinkles and puckers as I salivate. Dizzie brings down the knife.

Arla wheezes as the cold steel enters her chest. Her blood begins pooling around her. The boys start removing the chains from her body and gag from her mouth, certain they are no longer needed.

I take my first bites. As pack leader, I earn the freshest meal.

I nibble, savoring the taste and trying to fight the ravenous urge to eat fast, knowing my stomach will fill quickly. The others transform. I am quickly surrounded by four small dogs, gnawing Arla to the bone at her limbs.

"Enjoy... stardom," Arla sputters, quietly.

Five heads cock in confusion.

Arla's free hand moves up to her chest, finger tapping her cat brooch.

"Always... on guard." She grins, blood in her teeth.

A camera? She's recorded the whole thing. Should've known... should've known! Would someone have been watching? Do people really enjoy following the neighborhood busybody on livestream?

My gut—filled with Arla—says yes.

Arla dies. Toenails clack on the ground as we all pace, knowing we are done for.

We really screwed the pooch.

THE PROP

See that guy being ripped in half, held high above the big guy's head? That's me, in all my intestine-flopping glory. Ed the Shred, one-half of the Strong Guy routine—the better half, if you ask me. But the best half, that's my upper torso, complete with a white-toothed grin as my bottom bits fall to the floor. I'm all about halves, you see? I've spent the better half of my life being torn apart only to lace my parts back together again in a couple days, ready for the weekend show. Half over here, half over there, while the crowd goes wild.

I found out about my special nature by accident. I was ten years old, playing in the cornfield. Nothing good ever happens in a cornfield and this was par for the course. I had my little army men doing a full-blown siege of Vietnam, and I was deep in jungle territory. My head was in the trees, wasn't paying attention none to the sounds around me. Guns were blasting too loud in my tiny brain. I didn't hear it when the thresher motored up the row I was belly-down in, and I didn't even hear the slopping of my guts go flying as the metal blades churned me into pieces higher than I could count to.

Mom was real shaken. It was her turn to groom the fields and I highly doubt she was expecting the blood spray that came down my special little war row. But Mom was torn to bits inside after she rolled over her little Eddy. Her bits came back together though, when she started noticing my pieces moving back together after sitting in the field for an hour or two in shock. Turns out I'm a regenerator, sort of. Not really making new pieces, like a starfish or something, but more kinda magnetizing myself back together.

What a way to find out I'm special, eh?

Mom couldn't have been more thrilled to have me back together—even the little pieces that had clung to her face found their way back into my body. Self-cleaning makes me even more of a prize. Dad, though, he was messed up finding out what I could do. He sent me off to the literal circus faster than you can say "clown" and I've been here ever since. He didn't want a freak, but thankfully the circus loves them.

You can read all about my story on the back of your popcorn bag there, along with all the other charming people in the circus. They've got me next to my partner, Jed the Strong Guy. Some people think he's the real star of the show, since he does the ripping and tearing. Some people just call me the prop. They don't think I could possibly be real, even though this circus is full of things that shouldn't exist, but do. But Ed the Shred, the amazing immortal man, being ripped in half every few days, is just too unbelievable I guess. Oh well. I know my place. I don't just make the Strong Guy look good. I'm the strongest guy there is. Who else could verifiably die every few days only to stitch himself back together? Just me. And I look damn good with a little twirly mustache, even when it's halfway across the ring.

I'm the most put-together guy there is. Just the prop? That's only half the story, and like I've been telling you, I'm the best half there is.

Brian reached down to pick up the torso. Ed the Shred was heavy, even at half his normal weight, so the seventeen-year-old had to dig into the ground to heft him up and sling him across his back. Ed wrapped his arms around Brian's neck and the two made their way towards the large circus tent in the middle of the cornfield.

"So what do I win?" Brian asked, voice strained under Ed's weight.

"Whatever you want, kid," Ed replied.

"Whatever?"

"Yeah, I mean within reason of course. Infinite popcorn, a year's supply of tickets, an internship at the circus. You name it."

"Does this happen often?" Brian asked, tripping over a stray rock.

"You mean does Jed get mad, rip me in half, and toss both parts of me in separate directions into the cornfields?" Brian was silent. "Yeah, it sure does. Doesn't usually happen in the middle of a show though."

"As long as you know the way back," Brian said.

"Hey, that's your job," Ed retorted.

Brian paled. "I…"

"Just kidding, kid. I know these fields like the back of my hand, and luckily both of those are still attached. You just carry me and walk. There, take a left at that stalk of corn."

"Which stalk?"

"Any of them, just turn left."

The two of them carried on, making their way back to the circus tent in the distance. Ed thought about the last hour of his life, slowly building in anger as he grew more embarrassed, wondering who had control of his bottom half.

In the middle of the show, Ed had pushed the wrong button, made the wrong sly comment under his breath at Jed the Strong Guy's expense. Instead of taking it on the chin, Jed ripped Ed in half—all part of the routine—until he launched both sides of Ed through the roof of the tent in different directions. The ringleader had acted fast, announcing a contest for the first two people who brought Ed back to the tent. His pieces may have found their way back together eventually, but the ringleader knew how much a little contest could do for a struggling circus.

Brian, after searching the cornfields for the better part of an hour, had stumbled across Ed's upper torso, complete with his talkative head.

"I'm glad you found me, Bobby."

"Brian."

"I'm glad you found me, Brian. Wonder who got the bottom half. Hope it's a hot blonde. You like a hot blonde?"

Brian blushed, thinking about the cute boy he had spotted across the aisle in the circus tent. "I've been known to like a few."

"Well, let's hope for both our sakes it's a hot blonde."

Ed continued yammering as the two trekked through the cornfields, the sun beginning to set.

"He really tossed you far out, didn't he?"

"Sure did. I'm surprised you found me."

"Got lucky I guess," Brian said, shrugging. "Figured by the height of your arc you had to be around here somewhere."

"Well I'm glad you were able to calculate your way to me. Let's hope you can stay lucky. And we get back soon. Any chance you can pick up the pace? The clowns are coming out soon to keep the scarecrows in check."

Brian stumbled as his heart clenched. "What?" he squawked.

"You know, the clowns with knives, the scarecrows and their sickles. All that jazz."

Brian paled considerably.

"I'm just kidding, Bobby."

"Brian."

"I'm just kidding, Brian. Just trying to motivate you."

"I see the tip of the tent. We're almost there."

"Thank God," Ed said.

A murder of crows burst from the crops, startling Brian. "What was that?" he said, trembling.

"Probably nothing. Probably just scared of us."

"I hope that's the case."

Ed adjusted his grip around Brian's chest. "Probably."

Another twenty minutes passed, and finally, the two crossed the threshold of the circus tent. Brian pushed the flap of the tent back and walked through, Ed still squarely on his back. The ringleader approached the two.

"Ah," the ringleader said. "I see you've stumbled across the top. The legs have just arrived as well. You can place him over there." He gestured towards the center of the tent. The crowd had cleared out hours ago. Brian shuddered at how empty the tent felt, how spacious and overwhelming it was. He looked upwards and saw the two pinpricks of light where Ed had flown through earlier. Then, he turned his attention to the center of the ring, where a lone pair of legs were sat on a platform.

Brian walked up, surprised to see the blond boy he'd seen during the show. He looked tired, worn from carrying the bottom half of Ed the likely miles he had taken him.

"Hey," Brian said, huffing as he gently placed Ed's torso onto the platform. "I see you found Ed's... better half."

"You kidding me? I'm laying right here!" Ed protested.

Brian ignored the half-man, having tired of his incessant chatting on the walk. "How was the journey?" he asked the boy.

"Well, despite the fact that there were two pairs of legs, and only one of us was walking, it wasn't so bad. Long. But maybe worth it? Any word on a prize?"

"Ed said anything we wanted, but I'm not sure he was really in a prime position to negotiate honestly." Brian reached his hand toward the boy. "I'm Brian, by the way."

"Jerry," the blond boy responded, shaking his hand. Brian's hand felt electric, a rush of feelings making his face flush. Jerry met his gaze, then looked away shyly.

The ringleader walked up. "Thank you to both of you for bringing Ed back together. He would have made it here some way or another, but this is much less messy. Wanna see the magic work?"

The two boys nodded and turned to face Ed, whose parts had already begun stitching themselves back together. It was incredible seeing the flesh weave together, like destruction in reverse. Ed the Shred really was way more than just a prop.

With Ed back together, the boys looked at the ringleader expectantly.

"Ah! About that prize. You are, after all, the contest winners." The ringleader stroked his beard thoughtfully. "I'd offer you cash, but we don't have much of that around these parts, despite how magical this show is."

The two boys looked at each other, feeling a blush around their cheeks.

"How about a private show?" the ringleader offered. "Free food, behind-the-scenes, the whole shish-ka-bob."

The boys nodded eagerly, excited to see the rest of the show and all the inner workings.

The ringleader smiled at them. "Okay then, I'll start the preparations." He tipped his hat and walked away, leaving Brian and Jerry to themselves.

"A private show, cool," Brian said.

"Yeah, always wanted to see how it all goes down. And free peanuts, too!" Jerry replied, laughing.

"I suppose it's not the best prize for carrying half a man through a cornfield for a couple hours."

"No, it really isn't," Jerry agreed.

"We could, you know, spice it up," Brian said, hand rubbing the back of his neck.

"What're you thinking?" Jerry asked.

"Wanna make it a date? I'd love to get to know the guy that carried a pair of legs through a maze of corn."

Jerry's face turned red. "Yeah, yeah. I'd like that."

The two boys smiled, excited for the prize.

As it turns out, Ed the Shred really can bring the parts—the best parts—together.

I INK, THEREFORE I AM

From wall to wall, people buzzed about the office floor. Like every Tuesday night, the building that housed Electro-Sure, the premier insurance company for large-scale electronics, nearly glowed against the skyline. Long past the end of the day, Dario didn't even notice that he was pushing into his third hour of overtime for the evening. There were papers to be stamped, after all.

July was one of their busiest months. Employees swarmed over files like flies on hot molasses, trying to find last-minute loopholes in insurance policies before closing out the fiscal year. Dario felt sweat dripping down his back, the weak and broken office fans doing nothing to penetrate the summer heat as he poured over paperwork, numbers blurring together.

Dario wasn't sure how he was going to last another night, especially *this* night, with his sanity. His vision had him seeing triples of numbers, making nonsense words of letters. He needed a break, but he couldn't take one because his overlord of a boss was watching their every move, making sure they danced the perfect mating call ritual between their pens and countless insurance documents.

Confined to his desk, Dario did as he always did when the going got rough: he focused his attention on the dark, black stain on the ceiling, a reminder that things could be so much worse than they were.

Dario remembered the first time he'd heard watercooler talk about what caused the ever-growing stain, milky black like the night sky though polluted haze.

"They say it's where Mr. Eddson incinerates you on the spot if you misfile too many papers."

"It's mold from the boiling hot pot the boss has up there, ready to cook you in your own juices if you do something to lose a client."

"Asbestos, probably."

Nothing quite like the sweet queen of office gossip to keep the bees motivated. Whatever it was, it offered a spot of solace in Dario's day. Something to do that wasn't staring at a screen, inputting the umpteenth row of numbers into a spreadsheet. Something that didn't require smooth-talking clients into selling their soul to save a few extra bucks on their policies.

Dario had sold his own soul to this job for five years now. When he'd first sat in his chair at the cubicle, leaned back trying to soak in what he thought was the good life, he'd seen that stain for the first time. It was small then, a mere inch in diameter, but still standing out against the white ceiling and fluorescent lights.

Since, it had grown to a solid foot across, darker at the edges, filled in, then moving out once again. At the end of each fiscal year, with a fresh round of layoffs, the spot filled the void of the ceiling tile bit by bit.

Dario didn't think they were really related, despite the chat around the office, but Dario also didn't think he would have stayed at this awful job for as long as had; yet here he was. Pushing paper, breaking pencils, making people cry when their insurance payouts never came at the whim of his pen and company.

Up he looked, wondering what his ceiling panel Rorschach test had in store for him today. Blackness stared back at him, daring him to find an image in its design. All Dario saw was a dark cloud above him, ready to rain down until he could clock out for the day.

Sighing, Dario pulled his gaze away from the stain on the ceiling, hoping to get home at some point tonight. He had wrestling to watch, after all, and a TV dinner calling his name.

"All right, ants. We're going to be here all night and probably all day tomorrow," his boss, Mr. Eddson said from above them all, out the window of his office. "Too many accounts still need closing out and you worms are barely moving at a snail's pace."

"Excellent motivation," Dario's work partner and best office friend, Julie, mumbled, nudging him in the ribs. Dario fought back a grin.

"I love when he compares us to every insect," Dario said.

"Dario! I'm watching you extra close this year. Still plenty of time to cut back on one last labor cost for next fiscal year."

"Of course, sir. All accounts will be reconciled no problem."

Mr. Eddson responded by slamming his door closed, shaking the weak cubicles on the office floor.

The momentary silence of Dario's co-workers in the presence of their demanding boss was broken as fresh chatter erupted throughout the office, shaken much like the cubicle walls.

Dario opened his mouth to say something insulting about Mr. Eddson to Julie, but he was interrupted by the feeling of something dripping onto his face. Dario's hand rose, prodding the substance. Something black and sticky stuck between his fingers. He looked up, noticed the black smudge on the ceiling collecting several drips of liquid, the rattling of the office having shaken one free.

After rolling the liquid between his fingers, it occurred to Dario that the stain he'd contemplated for the last five years of his life might be ink. The liquid certainly left a mark like the familiar substance, had no tangible foul odor. Dario's thoughts ping-ponged between convincing himself that it was indeed ink and not some other toxic substance that had leeched onto his skin, and wondering how a puddle of ink that big could perpetually sit in the same place.

The mystery ink, like all of life's greatest wonders, would have to wait. All he could do was rifle through a forest's worth of paper, which was staring menacingly at him from his desk. The all-nighter wouldn't be any less all night no matter how much he distracted himself.

And so he stamped, logged, and filed his insurance reports, his head empty as he worked, feeling like he must be sleeping a hundred micro-sleeps in a row on his feet. Julia did the same in the chair next to him, the wheels squeaking every time she leaned back to whisper a joke in his ear.

Dario finished his current pile of papers, wedged in manila folders, and took a deep breath. He looked to the ceiling, daring it to drip, but nothing fell from above. He found himself mesmerized by the stain once again, the black ink boring into his soul, asking him who he was. His silent reply was that he was just a cog in a really awful machine, its machinations designed to only make a profit.

Turning back to his work, Dario was interrupted by a loud bang upstairs as Mr. Eddson opened his door with so much force it damn near broke the wall.

"Julie!" The faces in the office paled, knowing what was coming. "Upstairs. Now!"

Julie turned a little gray in the face, turned to Dario and placed a hand on his arm. "I'd say it's been nice to know you, but the only reason I do is because of this thankless job." He couldn't look her in her eyes, kept his gaze on her fingers, nails painted bright red.

She stood up, straightened her slacks, and walked up to Mr. Eddson's office without another word. Dario wished he'd have said something comforting, had at least commented on her choice of nail polish, but he knew that tone of voice, dreaded the day that it came for him. Best just to let it happen quickly.

The entire office heard the words exchanged. Dario would even bet the grubs wriggling beneath the tacky brown carpet that Mr. Eddson compared them all to so often heard their boss tear into Julie. The admonishing for misplacing an important case file (it wasn't) and losing them a reason to deny a payout (she hadn't) and almost costing him the company (the company would be just fine, though Dario wouldn't have minded if it did go under, which would save him from having to gather the gumption to quit an unquittable job).

Dario knew he wouldn't see her again. The way employees were fired certainly didn't help with the concoction of wild stories. Mr. Eddson always had them leave from the back exit, through a door that opened out into an alley. They all called it the "unglory-hole". Nothing good ever came of its use.

A door slammed somewhere upstairs, and Dario knew the deed was done. He tried to bury himself in the work in front of him, hunched over the papers, reading endless entries about fried electronics. He made it all of three words before he felt a liquid drip onto his neck, causing him to arch his back and his lip to curl in disgust at the slimy feeling.

"Ach!" he cried out. An office mate asked him if he was okay. He spared a glance at the ceiling, a steady pace of drips falling from above. "Sorry, back spasm or something. I'm going to hit the head."

He took the opportunity to saunter to the bathroom, wondering why the ink was dripping so badly, and fought off the notion that it had something to do with Julie.

Dario ran the tap, letting the clear water swirl around the soap-stained bowl before cupping a bit in his hand and bringing it to the back of his neck, trying to wipe off the black smudge. His hand came away black, the ink moving into the whorls and arches of his fingerprints.

He gripped the edges of the sink, stared into his reflection. Noted his red eyes and tired expression, wrinkles permanently etched into his face. If he ever smiled again, it would be a miracle. He sure would miss having Julie around, the only one to crack the gray disposition of the office.

Dario examined his skin further. Dry despite the humidity in the office, acne blotting the sides of his nose. He looked past the red in his eyes, and deep into his pupil, the blacked-out spot looking deader than ever, no spark of light. His very own inkblot trapped in his vision.

He wished he could see inside himself. Think for himself. Be something other than the number of files he'd closed and lives he'd ruined.

But alas, back to the office to ruin some more.

Dario traipsed back to the cubicles, feeling immediately uneasy as the eyes around him gawked at his form. He caught a few glances his co-workers sent his direction before they darted away, pretending they weren't watching him walk the gallows walk back to his desk. Based on the necks craning in his direction, he knew he was a dead man.

"Dario!" a voice boomed from above. Mr. Eddson didn't even bother to open the door to scream his name and demand his presence.

Before heading upstairs to meet his fate, Dario took one last look at his desk. At the chair that had held him captive for five years of his life. At the files that seemed to take on a life of their own, growing in size and never depleting.

And finally, at the black ink stain, dripping steadily, nearly pouring from overhead. If the other workers noticed, they sure didn't let on. Dario scoffed. Don't ask, don't tell, don't help, don't ever do a damn thing you aren't told to do.

Dario gathered his jacket, ready to be kicked out to the curb. Gathered his favorite pen and pocketed a pad of sticky notes as his final middle finger to the office life. Gathered his courage to walk up the stairs. Gathered some semblance of relief that his time here was finally over.

Up he went, walking the creaky set of stairs to Mr. Eddson's office. He felt the eyes that followed him, no need to look away as they remained unacknowledged.

He opened the door, an entry that felt more like an exit; a first step towards a new—and better—life.

Mr. Eddson hunkered behind his desk, his slender form and horn-rimmed glasses casting a steely glare in Dario's direction. Dario found himself lost in those eyes, noting the same lack of life he had just witnessed in his own pupils staring him down behind glass panes.

"Sit," he barked, low and rumbly, a voice that seemed contradictory to his thin figure.

Dario obeyed, feeling the courage he'd gathered not moments before spilling from his fingertips, leaving his body through his mouth, lip quivering in fear, through his eyes, watering from the dry heat.

"I didn't want to have to do this," Mr. Eddson started.

Here it comes, Dario thought, already trying to figure out what line he wanted to use to reply to his boss, to try and show him he was in charge of his own life and that he didn't need this measly paper-pushing—

"But you've seen."

Dario raised an eyebrow, unprepared for the statement. "What?" was all he managed to squeak out.

"The ink," Mr. Eddson said. He pointed upwards. Dario's head followed Mr. Eddson's finger. "No you, idiot, the spot above your head."

Mr. Eddson rose from his luxurious brown leather chair. He stepped into the space between Dario and his desk and raised his arms. Dario flinched, but Mr. Eddson reached past him and to the back of his chair, spinning him 180 degrees.

Dario blinked. Rubbed his eyes trying to process what he was seeing.

He was right about the ink. The perpetual puddle. In front of him stood a vat, a yard in diameter, seeming to drop into the floor, through the floor, and Dario wondered how the bottom didn't burst through the ceiling above his cubicle.

Dario stood. Walked toward the vat to investigate the bubbling pool of dark: a void to nowhere. His eyes fixated, focusing on the object in the center, what looked like two hot dogs rolling in the inky bubbles.

Closer he got, when the red caught his eyes. The red of a polish, tipping the fingers of a friend he thought had left the building.

He gagged.

"The lifeblood of this company. The signatures on our contracts. It's all you. Perform well, you keep your place at the desk. Perform poorly, fuel the tank." He pointed to the cauldron. "Either way, you're always a part of the company. They never even see you truly leave."

Dario felt the hair on his neck stand straight, sensing the danger he was in. But the ink called to him. He faced the black liquid, trying to catch his reflection in its surface. He saw nothing. Just like he felt.

"As you know, the fiscal year is ending. I still have a few more costs to cut. I thought I could do it elsewhere, but the ink marked you, so I'll just cut a little more on labor this year."

Dario remained riveted to the black ink before him. Churning. Waiting for a pen to dip into it, sign a contract, a policy. Written in stone, written in blood, written in ink. Binding for all eternity. He gazed for what felt like the entire night, his overtime burning behind him. He saw nothing, saw nothing, saw nothing… then saw himself.

He placed his hands on the edges, placed a foot on the lip, and stepped forward.

Sinking, feeling the body of his co-worker in the vat with him, slowly boiling into the substance that littered the company's papers with curses.

"We appreciate your continued service. Thank you from the bottom of my—"

Dario heard nothing as his head sank below the surface.

DUGOUT

The town was silent. The warm air, wafting through the trees, swirling clouds of dust from the floor of the dry forest, smelled like sulfur. The summer had started, and it wanted blood.

The leftovers would bring her to it.

Of that, it was sure.

"Anton, hey, Anton," Vanessa called impatiently, tugging at his shirt.

"Yeah?" Anton replied, shifting his hat lower on his head, shielding his face from the hot summer sun.

"Did you see the moving truck?"

"Over on Fairweather Lane, right?"

"I'm so pumped. I saw bikes, and boxes marked with sports equipment. Do you think she can play?"

"She?" Vanessa was so good at being nosy these days.

"Yeah, I heard the neighbors talking about a daughter."

"Huh. Well, let's hope she can. Better baseball than the dam."

"Or the cornfields."

"Oh, and Hool's Hill."

"Don't forget about the Crooked Treehouse."

"You're right, that was a bad one." Kids really had the worst luck in this town. "C'mon, Vanessa. Let's go round up the crew," Anton said. He tried not to think about the way each new arrival had fallen. Silent tragedies that the town kept quiet. Nothing like high death rates for children to scare away new neighbors.

The two kids hopped on their bikes and pedaled off down the road. They barely noticed how the ground curved, how teeth clacked beneath the asphalt below. Like an old twitch of an eye, the remaining youth of Shover's Valley, the small town that sat like a wart on the face of a mountain, were no longer troubled by the way the earth breathed. They didn't even fear when the ground opened up to take some meat between its lips. They were far past taking, as it was.

The warm days, where the sun stays out to play late into the evening, infused the kids with a spark of life so infrequently felt throughout the school year.

Another summer, another new kid.

Anton chuckled to himself, remembering the deaths of all the children before. *God, how this town will eat you alive*, he thought to himself. Fingers crossed it wouldn't take her.

"Charlene! C'mon, let's go! Get that tush in gear," Char's mom yelled out, her head poking inside the moving truck.

"I'm coming! That last box was heavy!" Char replied.

"Don't you even think about complaining about your back. You're twelve, for God's sake!"

"I said I'm coming, Mom," Char mumbled quietly to herself. She approached the moving truck, the family's belongings strewn about the yard. She picked up another box from the back and headed towards her room.

The end of the school year had come much too quickly for Char. While most kids were excited to start their summer and throw out old notebooks filled with gibberish schoolwork, Char had dreaded the end of school. With the academic year done, it was time to move to a new town. Her mom had promised her that the fresh start would be worth it. That making friends would be fun and that learning about the town would be exciting.

Char was skeptical. She had built her life in Sacramento, the bustling city a part of her history. A move to Shover's Valley halfway across the country in the middle of nowhere was bound to be a disaster. It wasn't her home. Char cursed her mother's new job. She had tried to sell it as a step towards stability. Better income, more time at home, bigger house.

Stability, schmamility, Char thought, tossing the box she had grabbed onto her bed.

From her bedroom, she heard the sound of kids' voices out front, talking to her mom.

Maybe the friend thing won't be so hard, she thought to herself. Char smoothed her hair into her ponytail, straightened her shirt and headed downstairs.

In her front yard, a group of kids had parked their bikes on the lawn.

Okay, that's a LOT of new friends. Char cleared her throat and gave a little wave. Eight heads turned in her direction, all clad in baseball caps, gloves hung over their back, or in their bike baskets.

"Oh, Char," her mom said. "I unpacked the last box from the truck and look who I found hiding back there."

Char groaned, rolling her eyes.

One of the kids stepped forward from the pack, a boy with hair cropped close to his head, peeking out from under a blue baseball cap. He wore a striped t-shirt, the orange color contrasting vibrantly with his dark skin. His eyes held a kind wisdom to them, something that felt to Char far beyond his adolescent experiences.

"I'm Anton," he said, offering her a hand. She took in how cold his skin was compared to her own, burning hot against the rising sun. He must have sensed her noticing his chilly skin. "You get used to the heat around here at some point."

"I hope so," Char said. "Is every day a scorcher like this one?"

"Only the good days," a blonde girl from behind Anton replied. "Vanessa," she said, offering her hand as well, also cold when Char grasped it.

Anton held up his baseball mitt. "We've got a game coming up in a bit. We are heading to the field now. You play?"

Char shook her head. "Not well."

"That's okay," Vanessa said. "None of us are great. But if you come on out, we'll finally have a full team for the first time."

Char looked at her mom, who had returned to the lawn after moving in a few more items.

"Hey, Mom? Can I go play baseball with them?" she asked pointing her thumb at the kids.

"Well, as luck would have it, I just put the sports equipment box in the garage. And, your bike survived the trip unscathed. If all of your stuff is in your room, go ahead."

"Thanks, Mom," Char said, smiling. She ran off to the garage, rifled through the box to find her mitt, and hopped on her bike. "I'll be back for dinner!"

"You better. Be safe!" her mom yelled at her retreating form.

Char raised her hand to wave goodbye and rode off.

As the kids approached the baseball diamond, deep in the thickets of Shover's Valley, the air shifted. The earth sniffed, recognizing the scent of new blood approaching, and its mouth watered, filling the bubbling river with a surge of fresh liquid.

Rocks shuffled on the face of a mountain, cascading downwards, disturbing the crows below. The black birds flew off, cawing at their disruption, and through their mouths, the Shover's Valley laughed, joyously anticipating its impending meal.

With a rumble, it migrated deep beneath the earth to the field at the center of the land, following the scent of the collected youth.

Anton, Vanessa, Char, and the gaggle of children threw their bikes onto the ground when they reached the baseball diamond, a cloud of dust floating through the air.

The field was full of weeds and rocks, but it was still incredible to Char that it existed, like a glorious blank spot stamped into the surrounding thicket. It even had a set of dugouts—better than a rickety bench exposed to the hot summer sun.

The nearly twin dugouts were evenly spaced on either side of home plate, a thin wire fence separating them from the diamond. The planks of wood were worn and rotted, and Char could count at least three elaborate, dusty, heavy spiderwebs stark against the sun.

That's odd, Char thought, noticing the differences between the dugouts at her distance. She took in how one dugout had been spray-painted bright red inside, while the other was marked in a black paint. Char jumped when she realized the murky black dugout was occupied.

A second group of children were sitting together in the wooden structure.

The children sat in silence, pale in the shade of the enclosed space. Char couldn't help but notice that they looked… sick. Dark circles under their eyes, cracked corners of their mouths, shallow breaths—or were they even breathing at all?

"Are they okay?" Char asked, nearly whispering her question to Anton.

"Don't let them fool you. They're stiff competition around these parts."

"They barely look like they can lift their arms to hold a bat or throw a ball," Char replied, unsure of what she was getting herself into.

"They'll be fine. Promise. Once the game starts, you won't even notice."

"Notice what?" Char asked, but Anton had already walked to the pitcher's mound. Char squinted her eyes at the dugout again, and the eerily silent children began to pour out, warming up for the baseball game.

Char felt a cold hand on her shoulder.

"We're really glad you could join us," Vanessa said, a smile on her face. "It's the inaugural summer game, and it's the first time we've had a full team in a while. The other team is playing one down."

"Again," Char said, "Don't expect any miracles. I haven't done more than a game of catch with my mom in over a year."

"We're just happy to have you fill the void," Vanessa said, teeth shining in the sun. "We hope to get to keep you. Have fun, y'know?"

Anton's team filtered into their positions, leaving Char with exactly one option: center field. She put on her mitt, enjoying the cold sensation inside the leather compartment.

The first of the other team took their place at bat. Anton threw a fierce pitch, and the ball flew past the kid before he even had a chance to think about swinging. Two more pitches ended the same way, and the first out of the game was fast complete.

The next girl up to bat was wiry, but her aim was true as she knocked a ball all the way out past the bases. Left field scooped the ball and tossed it to Vanessa at second base, who fiercely tagged the girl.

The game continued, back and forth for at least an hour, the sun reaching its peak for the day, scorching Char's arms. The runs were tied, and Anton was getting ready to throw another pitch to the team of pale children. Char's heart jolted when the pitch resulted in a hit clear out to center field where she was standing. The ball soared through the air, momentarily eclipsing part of the sun. Char ran towards it gloved-hand outstretched. She dove through the air and caught the ball.

She didn't land.

She fell.

Through the earth, crumbling beneath.

Her glove still gripped the white, stitched ball. She tumbled through the dirt, into the mouth of the baseball field. She heard nothing above her, felt nothing below her except for emptiness.

Darkness.

I take the things I want.

A voice, deep and guttural, surrounded Char in the black void she was suspended in.

You. New. Anew. Do I want you in death? Do I want your life? The others have provided. Bright souls who bring me fresh offerings. The others I've returned, a shell, a husk. The givers, the taken.

The darkness filled with light, though Char could see nothing. Nothing until it—the earth, Shover's Valley—she didn't know—forced images in her mind. She saw the opposing team of kids in succession in moments of peril. Dead, floating in the waters of a dam, crushed beneath a fallen treehouse, ripped apart by a thresher in fields of corn, tumbling down the side of a steep hill. Over, and over they died. Over, and over, Shover's Valley had taken.

A choice. Die and live forever. Live, but die a servant.

Char didn't know what to choose, *how* to choose. So she did the only thing she could: float and scream. Her mouth opened, but no sound came out. Like so many other things, her voice was lost to the void.

She cursed internally, damning their move, her new friends, her crappy luck. She spat and roiled inside, angry and becoming herself a spot of darkness within the ever-black void.

A choice. No choice. We choose.

A thousand voices wailed around her, like an abysmally long echo, turning back on itself repeatedly, tripping over the tone that crossed its path. Char felt her consciousness slipping, only to jolt from a slap to her brain, bouncing off her skull.

She knew not what her fate would be, only hoped that her current state would be short-lived, and she could escape the purgatory of the bowels of Shover's Valley.

The voices continued their hellish chant, stuffing the space between her ears with what felt like wads of cotton. But with the voices, a story.

She heard how Shover's Valley consumed. Grew its own community on the backs of children. How summer comes and goes, each year, with another child taken, forgotten by their parents. She learned of the unnamed gap beneath the crust, where *it* lived and sat in silence—where she was now, she assumed. She listened, and she knew her place.

Choice, the voice boomed around her, through her, in her. *Choice. What. Will. You. CHOOSE?!*

There was a clap, like thunder rolling into an earthquake, and her world went darker still. Inside and out there was nothing.

The earth spat her out.

In the middle of center field, Char lay sprawled in the dry, dusty grass. The ball she had caught, what felt like centuries ago, tumbled from her glove. She heard it crunch as it rolled towards her head and stopped an inch short of her ear.

The sun beat down on her, but she no longer felt its heat.

She got to her feet. From her place in the field, she could see the kids split into their dugouts, an empty space in each wooden rectangle.

Anton, Vanessa, and the living. A life of servitude to the force beneath her feet.

The cold, the pale, and the dead.
A choice.
She walked to the dugout and took her seat.

THE CREEPUS

Jerry stared across the gap at Mike's sleeping form. He dared not move for fear of waking his twin, but he couldn't prevent his eyes from widening at the thin wisp of smoke rising from the cracks between their twin-sized beds, slithering and curling before disappearing.

This wasn't the first time something had floated up from the crack while Jerry lay awake late into the night. Or was it early in the morning? Jerry didn't quite know; he only comprehended how the time felt in between, much like the location of the arriving anomalies. In between.

Like the other few nights Jerry had seen the strange, displaced air, he convinced himself it was a trick of the light, or lack of light (there it was again, that in-between that Jerry couldn't put his finger on), and closed his eyes to fall back asleep again, dreaming of giant monsters and robots, plans for his toys later that day. Mike would continue sleeping peacefully, oblivious to his brother's plights, but all the while ready for his sibling to join him in their dreams of big action and adventures. With both sets of eyes closed, the smoke continued to billow from nowhere.

At eight years old, Jerry and Mike were full of energy. Each morning, they awoke ready to run their favorite action figures to their backyard to concoct wild stories of daring feats. Underwater rescues in their pond, Mars explorations on the hillside—barren of plant life with stony slopes—and massive city takeovers in concrete jungles constructed with large building blocks.

On the fifth day in their new home, the schedule was no different. Naomi and Wilton had moved to the small town of

Lemon Grove for the new job opportunity that had presented itself to Naomi's burgeoning pastry business. Lemon Grove was a modest town with much cheaper living costs, and it felt like the kind of place a family could lay down its roots. There were trees—miles of them—a stark difference from the loud city where they had lived before. With Jerry and Mike so young, Naomi and Wilton felt that they could help the boys build their lives, barely noticing the disruption around them. They had each other, of course. And each other, for twins, was everything.

The boys were used to hearing noises at night. Horns honking, tires screeching, sirens wailing, and the distant sound of ever-moving cars provided the white noise the twins could fall asleep to. So now, in their rural home, Jerry and Mike found themselves unable to sleep as soundly, faced with the distractingly silent nature of the quiet around them.

The closeness of the twins was mimicked by the layout of their room, their play space wide-open on the right side of the room, and their beds pushed flush together on the left side, the foot of each bed perpendicular to the entryway. Naomi and Wilton felt it best to let the boys lean into the comfort the proximity gave them, especially as they settled into the new home. Wilton had been skeptical at first, not wanting his boys to be mocked later in life for their codependency, but Naomi convinced him that she had a plan. Gradually, the two beds would be moved further apart, until eventually they would flank either side of the room. Naomi knew her boys would buy into the design by making it a game and relying on their already incessant need for Mom's approval.

"When you feel brave enough, we'll move your beds just a little more. Mommy loves her brave boys, but brave is never about pretending. With me, there's no need to fake courage," she told them, each settled on a separate knee, wide, adoring brown eyes looking deeply into hers. Naomi knew that her words were probably beyond the boys' years, but they were as much for her as for the twins. "Every time you feel braver, we'll move your beds out a little further. Brave boys get treats, so we'll have an ice cream night, too. Rewards all around." The maturity of the boys for the parents, sweet desserts for the twins. Naomi chuckled and ruffled the boys' auburn, soft hair, kissed by the sun as they adventured.

The boys felt so brave, they started their progress on the night of that fifth day. Their beds, once fully pushed together, moved only slightly on this first occasion, no more than an inch separating the two beds adorned with dinosaur sheets for Jerry and little spaceships for Mike. Playing with their diecast cars late into the night by the light of their flashlights, the twins tuckered themselves out. They fell asleep fast for the first night since arriving, unburdened by the silence as their heads hit the pillow.

By the gentle glow of their octopus nightlight, the creepus was born.

Jerry and Mike had slept the entire night, a feat that made them feel like they'd be able to keep their mom proud (and keep getting ice cream). Had they known what had occurred that first night that the creepus came into existence, they would have smashed their beds back together themselves. Jerry had seen the smoke from the tear, black, curling, filling the room with dread. He'd thought it a trick of the eye at the time, but had he been awake at all last night, he'd have seen the smoke for it was—an existence longing to grow. The smoke was simply the signal of what had finally begun, last night, as the creepus truly opened.

"Mike, I can't find the astronaut," Jerry shouted from their room, getting ready to play in their spacious backyard another day. The hot summer days were becoming much more beloved when the twins realized they had so much room to play to their hearts' content, endless stories at their fingertips. The summer in the city had been spent inside, the streets too busy to walk safely.

Mike looked up at his brother's loud inquiry, his voice so much like his own, but unable to recognize it as eerily similar; voices never sound the same in your own head as they do to others' ears. "It's not out here!" he yelled back, after scanning the backyard for the white, puffy action figure.

The patter of Jerry's footsteps grew closer, his tiny figure approaching, arms overflowing with toys of various shape and function. His voice vibrated with each step, "Aw, man. Mike, he's my favorite. If you lost him, I'm telling Dad."

"I didn't lose him!" Mike defended himself. "Did you look under your bed? You put him there for guarding last night."

Jerry contemplated his actions and verified that he had in fact checked under the bed. "He wasn't there. I swear."

"No swearing," Mike retorted. He had heard his dad say that before.

"I don't think saying 'swear' is a swear," Jerry replied. Mike giggled, and the two ran off to play.

Back in their bedroom, the creepus heard their argument, and from the crack between their bed, a stocky, white astronaut figure clattered to the floor.

"Time for bed," Naomi sing-songed to her boys as she tapped their behinds, clad in matching spotted pajamas, and they ran to their room.

"Who do you want to stand guard tonight?" Mike asked.

"Let's put Chawy under there," Jerry replied. Mike nodded in agreement and grabbed his stuffed bear, ragged fur frayed by time and food and dust and the other generally unhygienic things that followed little boys. Mike crawled under the bed to place his totem underneath. Jerry heard his brother gasp.

"He's here!" Mike shrieked. "I told you so," he muttered, crawling backwards out from under the bed, holding up the astronaut toy proudly in his hands.

"No way!" Jerry yelled. "You put him there, didn't you?"

Mike's face turned to a scowl. "No, I told you, he was just under the bed where you put him. He's all dirty though," Mike continued, handing the toy over to his brother. He was right: the figure was covered in a layer of soot, the black marbling the white coat of paint.

Jerry flipped the visor up on the toy and let out an audible shocked inhalation. Where the astronaut once donned a confident smile, the figure's face had twisted into a horrified expression. Jerry dropped the toy at his discovery, the *thunk* of the figure clattering to the floor deafening as Mike awaited an explanation from his brother.

"Weird," Mike muttered, upon investigating the toy himself. He turned to Jerry, who had wide eyes filled with confusion. "I found him underneath that crack in our beds. That little space where they were pushed together."

"The creepus," Jerry said, under his breath.

"The what?" Mike asked.

"In my mind, it's called the creepus," Jerry repeated.

Mike nodded in agreement. "Me too. It sure is creepy."

"I thought I heard something the other night. Like gas," Jerry said, quietly. Mike snorted at the mention of gas.

"We're brave though. We want to be brave to make Mom happy and to get ice cream. Let's just put an extra guarder tonight, just in case." Mike walked across the room and grabbed his policeman toy.

"Just in case," Jerry complied.

Chawy the bear and the tiny policeman were placed on guard, under the bed, beneath the creepus. With the guards in place, the boys climbed into bed. Sleep fought them at first, but soon, soft breaths emerged in steady bursts and the twins were asleep.

From the creepus, the hand appeared. Long, almost tentacular, with fingers gnarled and covered in slime, the hand reached. Both boys were out of reach, so the hand retreated to the space between, disappearing before reappearing below the bed. The hand dragged on the floor, touching the soft, frayed bear and hard plastic policeman. The hand grabbed hold tight and slithered back into the empty space from whence it had come. Silently, the toys entered the portal.

Most of the night passed before the crack opened once more, and the hand deftly placed the toys back in their previous positions. The bear now bore fangs where a smile once lived, and if the boys were to pull the trigger on the tiny gun the policeman owned, they would find it now shot small, metal projectiles.

Like everything that comes to the creepus, it never returns the same.

Days passed, the boys played, their parents worked, and the creepus grew. Jerry and Mike were making substantial progress in their quest to sleep separately. Naomi had widened the space between their beds several times over the last week at a schedule that was faster than she had anticipated. It seemed the boys' appetites for ice cream greatly outweighed their need to be close.

Jerry and Mike had stopped placing guards underneath the bed after Chawy and the policemen. They were wary of the creepus, but they slept through the nights even as the hands reached for them. The hands became arms, and the arms became shoulders, and now, at midnight in the twins' room, a faceless head emerged from the creepus.

The body was colored like sour milk. White, but viscous. Impure.

The empty space between the beds, holding a portal that had no edges, no light, no announcement of its presence other than the figure stepping through its folds, was empty no more.

Dripping otherworldly sweat, the figure stretched from the creepus and reached for the sleeping boy, unaware of the presence hovering inches from his face. Long fingers touched the child, and brown eyes shot open, settling on the monstrosity before him.

A second pair of eyes fluttered open from across the gap, widening as the figure hunched over his brother. Sensing the new eyes on its back, the figure turned, staring with its empty face at the horrified boy, paralyzed in fear.

Before the boy could even move or try to wake his unsuspecting twin, the figure wrapped its victim in spindly, sticky arms and scooped him up. The bodies whipped back into the void, disappearing into the nothingness.

In the still of the night, Jerry sat, open-mouthed, feeling the loss of his twin deep within as soon as Mike was between the beds and gone. He wheezed through his loss, his lungs constricting in terror.

"Mom!" he squeaked out, high-pitched, the word choked out as loudly as he could. "Mo-om!" he shouted again, his frantic voice breaking, turning the single syllable into two.

Down the hall, a light turned on, and Naomi and Wilton jumped out of bed, hearts pounding at the sound of their son's terrified voice. They breached the boys' room, stopping just inside the threshold to see Jerry pointing at Mike's very empty bed. Tears streamed down his face.

Naomi rushed to her son. "What happened? Where's Mike?"

"He's in the creepus! It took him into the creepus!" he shrilled, pointing at the yard-length space between the beds.

"Wilton, don't just stand there, go look for Mike," Naomi admonished. Wilton stood there, stunned. Naomi, exasperated, waved her hand at the door. "The backyard, go!" She turned to Jerry. "Sweetie, where's your brother? Tell Mommy; it's okay."

Jerry hiccupped, and pointed again, agitated. "It took him there! The creepus, I told you."

Naomi huffed in exasperation. There was nothing between the beds, a fact that shouldn't have belied the truth, but the creepus existed nevertheless. "I'm going to go look in the bathroom and then the living room. He couldn't have gone far. Stay here. I love you," she said calmly, kissing her son's forehead.

With Naomi gone, Jerry felt the weight of the nothingness overwhelm him. It tore his heart to pieces inside—he had rarely been separated from Mike since, well, forever. The quiet rushed over Jerry, his face flushing, his breathing speeding up, and panic began in full force. He stared at the space where his brother should have been lying. He stared for what felt like hours, but in reality, was only minutes. Minutes, however, that soon saw a pair of pale hands emerging from nowhere. Unlike earlier in the night, they were full, carrying the still body of the young boy. It placed him in the bed before quickly retreating back into the void.

"Mike!" Jerry yelled, rushing to his brother. He rolled his twin over, and identical brown eyes stared back at him. "Are you okay? Where did you go?"

Mike continued to look at his kin. Jerry looked back, trying to determine if his brother was in fact his brother. Everything that came out of the creepus came back slightly off, but Jerry couldn't determine anything out of the ordinary.

Mike's voice cut through the silence. "I'm fine. I just went elsewhere, but I'm back now."

"What was it like?"

"It was like here."

"Are you okay?" Jerry asked for the second time, despite the fact that Mike had answered it once.

"I'm fine," Mike repeated.

Jerry questioned it internally again, and again. Even though his brother sat before him, seemingly untouched, he knew it to be a lie. He knew this from the way that he still felt like half of him was missing, in the beyond, in the *other*, away.

Naomi and Wilton returned shortly after Mike came back through the void. As they entered the room relief flooded their faces, seeing their son back in his bed where they'd kept hoping he'd be as their search had turned up nothing. They clamored to his side, wrapping him up in their arms.

"Where'd ya go, kiddo?" Wilton asked.

"I was just in the closet. I heard something and got scared," Mike responded.

"You didn't hear us come in? We were so worried," Naomi pried. Mike shrugged in response. Naomi sighed, "I'm just glad you're okay. Don't do that again."

Jerry kept quiet, afraid to mention the creepus again for fear of making his mom mad.

"Will you boys be okay to go back to sleep?" Wilton questioned. The boys nodded, and the parents gave them both one more kiss and left the room with a soft goodnight and whispered I love yous trailing behind them. They were shaken but didn't want their kids to be any more unnerved than they already seemed. Upon seeing their son where he belonged, after what seemed like a trivial mistake, they dared not make a bigger deal of the situation, setting their boys back on the bravery progress they'd made.

With the parents gone, Jerry and Mike continued their quiet stare down. Mike wordlessly got up from his spot, walking around to the other side of his bed. Heaving slightly, he pushed the wire frame of the bed towards Jerry's, the thin metal feet of the bed scraping along the hardwood floor, and the two were flush together once again. Jerry did not protest, hoping the proximity to his brother would ease his rapidly beating heart.

For now, nothing could go into the void, and nothing else would come out. The creepus was closed.

The next morning came slowly, as Jerry had been unable to fall back to sleep. He kept watching his brother, convinced he'd see a pair of wings or tail or set of fangs after his visit to the creepus. But morning arrived, and Mike awoke like every morning—a smile on his face, ready to greet the day with the gleeful exuberance kids are so quick to exhibit. There was play to be had, after all.

Jerry kept his watchful eye on his brother throughout the day, waiting for him to slip up, to be different than what he knew his brother to be, to show that he was not Mike, but rather the Mike from the creepus. He played like Mike, they trifled with each other like brothers, and his body looked the same as it has the night before. It wasn't until the boys were in for the night and changing for bed the Jerry saw it.

Mike took off his shoes, and as Jerry watched him slip the tiny cartoon-clad sneakers off his feet, he noticed the unusual shape of his toes. Once he removed the socks, he realized it wasn't just his toes, more oblong than usual, but also the nails: pointed, yellow, and thick. Jerry's eyes widened, and the little voice in his head simultaneously shrieked *I knew it!* while trembling in terror that his brother was not his own.

In that moment, Mike knew what he had to do. He had to be brave, not just for his mom, but for his whole family.

Naomi put the boys to bed, noting their already tucked-in presence when she came around for goodnight. She kissed the boys on the head, trying not to sigh in disappointment that their beds were shoved back together again, and left, turning their light-switch off and leaving them in the glow of the octopus nightlight.

With Naomi gone, Jerry took a deep breath and steadied himself for what he needed to do.

"Mike?" he asked, breaking the silence. "Can we move our beds back? I want to keep being brave."

He awaited his brother's response. Jerry was silent for a beat too long before responding, "I like it better this way, Jerry. Let's leave it like this."

"But if we move the beds, we can get ice cream tomorrow."

"I don't really want any ice cream."

Jerry sighed, unsure of how to proceed. Maybe... maybe brute strength would be the way. He popped out of bed, planting himself where the two mattresses joined, lifted, and pushed. His bed was close to the wall of the room, but he was able to nudge it slightly to the side, creating a crack between the beds. From that crack, black smoke began wisping upwards.

Mike looked like he was panicking, but he remained on his place in the bed, scrambling a bit further away from the growing creepus. With another heave, Jerry moved his bed with enough space to wedge himself between the mattresses. As soon as he had planted himself between the bed, part of him disappeared within, as unceremoniously as everything had moved between before.

Jerry knew he had one chance, so he moved fast. Mike flailed as he tried to move further from the portal. Jerry lunged. His small fingers closed around Mike's wrist, and he pulled harder than he thought was possible, and with that pull and all the fight he could muster, he tugged himself and his not-twin brother into the creepus.

It was strange, Jerry wondered, how it felt to be in between, *truly* in between time and space. His young mind wouldn't allow for total comprehension, but even a mind steeped in maturity and experience would be at a loss, trapped in a state of cataloguing the odd environment.

Inside the creepus was not what Jerry would have expected. Seeing those long, pale arms grab his brother the night before, Jerry would have thought this place would be dark, like a cave, filled with monsters who needed no sight, but only to feel around and *grab*.

Yet, the creepus was filled with a pulsating blue light, or at least something that passed as blue, as he floated, his fake brother beside him, to the creepus floor. When he finally hit the ground below, he bluntly bounced once, twice, before landing on a rocky abutment. Once at the bottom, he looked around and suddenly, his earlier expectations were met.

While he had traveled through the between state, between the normal—his world—and what existed in a pocket of that world, everything became light and quiet. But as soon as he landed, the darkness began, and so did the screams and growls and groans that, for the time being, had no apparent source.

Brave, he told himself again. *Be brave.* He looked to his side and saw that Other Mike was nowhere to be found. As soon as they hit the bottom, there was only Jerry.

Jerry called out, hoping to find his real brother. "Mike!" he shouted, his high-pitched youthful voice cutting through the deeper moans.

"Jerry!" he heard shouted back, from what sounded like hundreds of yards away.

Jerry stood up and sprinted in the direction of his brother's voice. Dark, dark, and more dark pushed inwards at him, surrounding him, suffocating him, but on he ran, shouting his brother's name as he did, imagining each of his brother's responses like beacons of light.

"Jerry!" he heard again, finally sounding closer. And soon, he began to feel it. That piece of him that was absent before, as soon as Mike had gone through the creepus, felt alive again at his twin's near presence. The darkness around him continued to feel impossibly black, but Jerry let the voice and his feeling guide him forward, until finally, he saw his brother huddled against a wall, knees pulled to his chest, his tiny frame trembling.

"Mike! Oh, Mike!" Jerry shouted before sidling up next to his brother, giving him a big hug. Jerry returned with his arms clutched tightly around his brother. Reunited, the two stood up and took in their surroundings.

"You've been missing since last night," Jerry explained. "And there was something there in your place. Just like the astronaut, and Chawy, and the policeman."

"So you came in?"

"I came in. And I took whatever was you in with me, but he's gone now. I don't know where he went."

"We gotta get out of here. Where's the door?" Mike asked.

"I didn't see one, but we came from up," Jerry replied, pointing to the vast section above them. Far away, in the distance from where Jerry had run from, they could see a tiny pinprick of light in the charcoal sky. "Maybe there?"

"Let's go," Mike nodded in agreement.

The two set off, back through the maze of the darkness, using the speck of light to guide their way. They stepped forward at a brisk clip, but before long felt something matching their pace. Something that loomed.

The twins heard the breathing, a wheeze, really, and felt the gusts of wind coming from the thing behind them on their necks. They picked up their stride, afraid to turn around. The wheeze grew louder, sounding like the respirator their grandma had been attached to in her final moments of life. Jerry chanced a look behind him and wished he hadn't.

Less than ten yards away, a giant astronaut hovered at the heels of the boys. It looked just like their action figure they'd lost in there days before, but larger than a life-sized scale would ever be. Behind his visor held a bulb full of red blood, ready to rush forward upon opening. Skeletal hands stretched forward, flaps of thick gloves hanging off the fingertips like leathered flesh.

The boys ran, beginning to sob, closer and closer to the space below the light. From the left, a second figure emerged, this one wielding a gun. The policeman toy that had previously guarded the bed now guarded their exit, he too larger than manageable, especially for the two young boys. The policeman pointed his revolver and pulled the trigger, three times in quick succession. The boys expected giant bullets to come flying forward, but instead the firearm shot balls of lint, tangled with fingernails and hair, all victims of the creepus condensed into tiny spheres of nightmarish proportions.

The projectiles shot by the policeman went over, behind, and over again, missing the boys each time by some luck of faith. They ran faster and faster still, their juvenile energy coming in handy in their time of need. The policeman loaded his gun once more, a grimace on his face, fangs jutting over his bottom lips, drawing blood from his own face, his body rejecting the unearthly proportions.

Mike tripped. Jerry felt his brother's hand slip through his.

Jerry jerked backwards, kneeling next to his brother. At that moment, the astronaut lunged and the policeman fired again. The boys ducked, making themselves as small as possible, and the astronaut, with his momentum, flew above them into the path of the incoming bullets made of detritus.

The condensed ball of human refuse, decay, and dirt hit the astronaut in his face, breaking his visor, sending forth a rush of frothy, viscous blood.

The boys took one look at the astronaut's skeletal face, revealed after the bubbling liquid had spilled from his helmet.

"Oh, God, oh, God, oh..." Mike repeated over and over.

"Get up!" Jerry yelled, jerking his brother to his feet. They were on the move again.

They were quickly approaching their exit, the bright pinprick of light glowing above them. It felt impossibly out of reach, but all they could do was run, terrified, shaking, sweating from their encounter with the monstrosities behind them, recovering from their mishaps.

"Agh!" Jerry sounded off suddenly, as a gigantic shadow came into view. Their favorite savior, Chawy, towered over them. No longer the cuddly bear he was before, spikes, bones, pipes, and other shards of various sharp things protruded from his back. He growled and then roared, and from behind him, dozens of the tall, pale, faceless creatures that had emerged from the creepus came rushing forward.

"Climb!" Mike shouted as the two approached the demon version of Chawy, seeing no other way to reach the light above then to traverse their furry enemy. The two gripped fistfuls of fur, smelling the fetid breath coming from the massive bear as they climbed. The bear was angry, but too uncoordinated and short-armed to reach the boys.

Jerry and Mike scaled the giant bear, the grimy fur slipping between their fingers at times, but their fearful movements making miracles happen as they managed to maintain their pace. The alabaster-colored, faceless creatures caught on and began climbing as well, their long bodies making their ascent faster than the twins'.

The boys were at the bear's chest, almost ready to crest the shoulders and make their final move to the head. The bear thrashed about, but the boys held on still. The faceless minions were right behind them, and the boys started to feel thin fingers grabbing for their pajama pants, the thin cloth ripping at weight of the hands.

On they climbed, ignoring the white-hot burning on their calves as the fingers began tearing their skin open, reaching their knees and occasionally their thighs, cutting hot rivulets into the boys.

"Go, go!" Jerry screamed as he elevated his brother with his hands, fingers weaved together to support his weight. Mike grasped the bear's pointed, dingy ear, then moved to his stomach to help hoist his brother up with him. The sharp hands waved below, rupturing skin when they made contact, a bloody path forged behind them on the hide of the enormous bear having done their damage as they mounted his body.

The twins reached the top of the bear's head, his roars deafening, hot air swirling around him. The light flickered above, their way out, back through the between of the creepus to their home and safety.

"We gotta jump!" Jerry yelled.

"It's too far!" Mike shrieked back.

"We have to!" Jerry resolved, urging his brother. "Jump!" he screamed, grabbing his brother's hand once more, pulling him towards the light. The boys jumped, and fell, up, up, up.

The pair breached the creepus, soaring through the glowing blue realm and finally, plunging abruptly back through the void and into their room, tumbling to the space between their beds. A hand reached up after them, elongating, stretching and grazing Jerry's shirt, but not quite gaining purchase of the cloth.

Without a word the boys ran to their beds and slammed them together, closing the entryway once again. A lone pale hand remained outside of the portal, cut off from its retreat. With the gateway closed, the hand appeared to freeze above the thin crack between the bed, still emitting black wisps of smoke, before thudding to rest on top of the bed, severed from its source. The hand was hardened and gnarled in a grabbing motion, but still in its movements. A memento from the creepus.

Jerry and Mike sat, out of breath, huddled in the corner of the room, as far from the creepus as they could be. They were alive, free from the in-between dimension they'd trudged through, the imagery bound to plague their nightmares.

Huffing, attempting to regain their breath, their mother's words echoed in their heads. *Mommy loves her brave boys, but brave is never about pretending.* They were alive, at least. But, like everything that enters the creepus, nothing emerges unchanged.

THE END?

Wait, there's more...

DarkLit Press Books

Dark Lines: Haunting Tales of Horror by Jack Harding

Slice of Paradise: A Beach Vacation Horror Anthology

Beach Bodies: A Beach Vacation Horror Anthology

A Note From DarkLit Press

All of us at DarkLit Press want to thank you for taking the time to read this book. Words cannot describe how grateful we are knowing that you spent your valuable time and hard-earned money on our publication. We appreciate any and all feedback from readers, good or bad. Reviews are extremely helpful for indie authors and small businesses (like us). We hope you'll take a moment to share your thoughts on Amazon, Goodreads and/or BookBub.

You can also find us on all the major social platforms including Facebook, Instagram, and Twitter. Our horror community newsletter comes jam-packed with giveaways, free or deeply discounted books, deals on apparel, writing opportunities, and insights from genre enthusiasts.

Acknowledgements

I am eternally grateful to my friends and family who have supported me in pursuing the things that seem daunting. Thanks to my mom and my partner Emmy for reading my stories and putting up with all the good and bad that comes with getting your work out into the world. To my friends, Jake, Devon, Alexis, Matt, Simmons, Kit, and Sophie— thank you for letting me ramble excitedly about each new endeavor.

This horror community has been a true treat to get to know. To all of the writing communities I have had the pleasure of being a part of, I thank you endlessly for your critiques, support, and for sharing your own work in an effort to help everyone grow. To the writers who have paved the way, thank you for making horror a safe space for those that identify at the margins. Thank you to Patrick Barb for reading this collection in its entirety and offering notes, and to those that believed in this manuscript along the way. Thank you to the publications who have previously published some of these stories. Every win along the way has made it easier to push on to the next.

Finally, thank you to DarkLit Press for this unbelievable opportunity and for putting together a beautiful book, to Truborn Design for the gorgeous cover, and to everyone else involved with making this book a reality.

Stay spooky and full of heart.

About the Author

Nikki R. Leigh is a queer, forever-90s-kid wallowing in all things horror. When not writing horror fiction and poetry, she can be found creating custom horror-inspired toys, making comics, and hunting vintage paperbacks. She reads her stories to her partner and her cat, one of which gets scared very easily.

She has stories published in Dark Matter Magazine, Ghost Orchid Press's Hundred Word Horror anthologies The Deep and Rock Band, Blood Rites Horror's Welcome to the Funhouse and Pulp Harvest, Dread Stone Press' Field Notes from a Nightmare, Ghost Orchid Press' Chlorophobia and Crystal Lake Publishing's Shallow Waters: Vol. 8, among other publications. Upcoming publications include poetry in Under Her Skin, and stories in The Book of Queer Saints, Cemetery Gate's A Woman Built By Man, Eerie River's It Calls From the Veil and Monsters & Mayhem, and Dead Sea Press' Terror in the Trench, among others.

Content Warnings

In *Recipe for a Disaster*:

Violence and self-injury.

In *That I Swallowed a Genie*:

Some description of gore.

In *Give to Take*:

Description of a hate crime and violence.

In *To Pluck a Seed of Sorrow*:

Death of family member.

In *Replenish:*

Self-image issues.

In *Next Day Delivery*:

Ex-stalking and violence.

In *The Pits*:

Anxiety issues.

In *Bear Hang*:

Violence.

In *Wolfpig, Show Me Your Teeth*:

Grief and implied harm to a child.

In *Doubling Down*:

Stalking and violence.

In *Pins and Needles*:

Self-injury.

In *Live! From Jekyll's Hideout*:

Harm to a child.

In *On the Same Wavelength*:

Gore.

In *The Slow Siege of Zenohtown*:

Gore.

In *Tiny Dog, Big Bite*:

Violence.

In *Dugout*:

Harm to a youth.

In *The Creepus*:

Children in peril.

DARKLIT
PRESS

Made in the USA
Middletown, DE
25 September 2022

11188611R00144